The Outfit

The Outfit

RICHARD STARK

The University of Chicago Press

The University of Chicago Press, Chicago 60637
© 1963 by Richard Stark
All rights reserved.
University of Chicago Press edition 2008

Printed in the United States of America

21 20 19 18 17 16 15   9

ISBN-13: 978-0-226-77101-4 (paper)
ISBN-10: 0-226-77101-6 (paper)

Library of Congress Cataloging-in-Publication Data

Stark, Richard, 1933–
     The outfit / Richard Stark.
           p. cm.
     ISBN-13: 978-0-226-77101-4 (pbk. : alk. paper)
     ISBN-10: 0-226-77101-6 (pbk. : alk. paper)   1. Parker (Fictitious character)—
Fiction. 2. Criminals—Fiction. I. Title.
     PS3573.E9O9 2008
     813'.54—dc22

                                                                 2008021509

♾ This paper meets the requirements of ANSI/NISO Z39.48-1992 (Permanence of Paper).

The Outfit

ONE

1

When the woman screamed, Parker awoke and rolled off the bed. He heard the *plop* of a silencer behind him as he rolled, and the bullet punched the pillow where his head had been.

He landed face down on the floor. His stubby, pregnant .32 was clipped to the springs under the bed like a huge black fly standing upside down, and Parker's hand was reaching out for it before he hit the floor. He spun a half-turn away from the bed and raised the .32 so the other one would know he had it but he didn't fire. This was a hotel room, and the .32 wasn't silenced.

A half-turn; then he reversed his spin and rolled under a bed, hearing the second bullet thud into the floor just behind him. His arms were tucked in close to his body and he rolled all the way across and came up on the other side, seeing the other one just stooping to fire under the bed. Parker threw the .32. The grip hit the other's forehead, just above the nose.

He grunted; then dropped out of sight. Parker bent and looked through under the bed. The other was lying on his face.

After the first scream, the woman had been silent. Now she stared, slack-faced, as Parker got to his feet and went around the bed. He was tall and lean with corded veins and hard, tanned flesh. His torso was creased by old scars. His legs had a bony angularity to them; the muscles were etched against the bones. His hands were big, thick, knotted with veins; they were made for gripping an axe, or a rock. When he picked up the .32 again, his hands made it look like a toy.

The killer lay, arms and legs splayed out, as though he'd been dropped from a height. His gun was still in his right hand. Parker stepped on the wrist, then bent and took the gun. It was a .25 caliber target pistol, useless for almost any serious work except to come up close and kill a sleeping man. The silencer had been made for a gun with a larger barrel, and a jury-rigged clamp arrangement had been fashioned to fit it to the small barrel of the .25.

Parker stuck his foot under the killer's chest, pushed, and rolled him over. He flopped over like a fish, his right arm swinging over and thumping the floor like a sack. He had a narrow pale face, skimpy eyebrows, small nose and thin lips, prominent cheekbones and temples. He wore a short-sleeved white shirt with button-down collar, a red-and-green striped tie, with sharply creased tan trousers with no cuffs, and highly polished brown shoes with zippers instead of laces. Floppy leather fringes hid the zippers. There was a purpling bruise on his right temple, and a small cut in the middle of it gleamed carmine. Parker had never seen him before.

The woman found her voice again and half-whispered, "Shouldn't we call the police?"

"Shut up a minute! Let me think."

It was a mess. She knew him as Charles Willis, absentee businessman with an income from a few parking lots and rental properties and gas stations here and there around the country. How to be square Charles Willis and explain a silent killer in the middle of the night? He had to give her a story; she had to be convinced by it; and it had to give her a reason to keep her mouth shut. The law, too, would want to know why a professional killer had been aimed at Charles Willis.

The truth might do it, but he didn't know her very well; nor how far he could trust her.

Her name was Elizabeth Ruth Harrow Conway. She was a good-looking woman, twenty-nine, with honey hair, golden flesh and the tall, lush, well-proportioned body of a voluptuous athlete. She lived on a combination of alimony from her ex-husband and atonement gifts from her parents. She'd always been rich, had always lived in luxury surrounded by servants, and she'd never had a problem that wasn't fashionable. That much Parker knew about her. Also, that she was fine in bed, and that she sometimes had a panther craving for brutality. He knew little more than that, and thought there was probably little more to know.

The killer made a small sound in his throat and his head thrashed slightly on the floor. His blond hair was dry and limp. Sweat had broken out on his face, though the room was air-conditioned. He'd be waking up soon, and Parker had to have the woman squared away by then.

He saw her watching him, and was surprised at her expression. He'd expected fear and astonishment, but she looked breathless. Pleased, excited, and curious. The way she always looked when they bedded together. Expectant. So, the truth. But as little of it as possible.

There was a wooden chair with padded seat and back over by the blind window, the one with the air-conditioner in it. He got it, brought it to the bed, and sat down. "Charles Willis isn't my name," he said. "I have another name. I use it in my work. You don't want to know about my work."

"What?" She frowned at him, and glanced down at the man lying on the floor between them. "I don't under——You aren't Chuck Willis?"

"I am now, and here. When I'm not working, I'm Charles Willis. Here in Miami, or in Nevada, or out on the Coast."

"And when you are working?" She'd absorbed it faster than he'd expected.

He shook his head. "You don't want to know that."

"But he——" She pointed at the man who had tried to kill him. "——he's from that other part of your life."

"That's right."

"What's his name?"

"I don't know. I never saw him before."

"Oh. You mean he was just hired."

"That's right."

"And you don't want to turn him over to the police."

"Right again."

"I see."

She reached out for the cigarettes on the night table. She was nude and, when she leaned to reach for the cigarettes, her breasts hung heavy for a moment. As she sat back again, they became firm again. She was a good animal.

She lit a cigarette. "I *don't* see. You aren't what you seem to be, but you don't want me to know what you really are. Whatever you really are, someone, somewhere, hired this man to kill you. Whatever you really are, it keeps you from wanting to be involved with the police. You want me to help you by being quiet, but you don't want to tell me what's going on."

He was silent. She studied him, frowning, but he had nothing to say. He sat and waited. While he waited he watched the killer, whose head had moved again but whose eyes hadn't opened yet. The bruise had stopped swelling, but it was an unhealthy color. The carmine outline of the small cut had started to dull toward maroon as the blood clotted.

After a minute Parker got to his feet. He had the .32 in his right hand, the silenced .25 in his left. He went over and put the .32 on the dresser, then went back and sat down, studying the thug again.

"All right," she said. "For now."

"Good."

She put her cigarette out, and nodded at the killer. "What about him?"

"We'll talk to him." He kicked the killer in the ribs. "You're awake," he said.

The killer opened his eyes. They were pale gray, gleaming faintly in the light from the table lamp on the night stand. His face was blank, as though he had no attitude about what had happened to him. He said, his voice as blank as his face, "You can't turn me over to the law. You can't kill me, because you can't get rid of the body and you can't trust the dame. And you can't kill her because that would bring the law on you. You got to let me go."

"You can trust me, Chuck," she said. Her voice was low. She was half-smiling as she looked down at the pallid face of the killer.

Parker ignored her. He said to the killer, "Name of your contact. The guy who fingered me."

The killer shook his head, rolling it back and forth on the floor, doing it carefully, as though he were part of a balancing act. His face was still blank. "No," he said.

"And the name of your contact in New York. You work out of New York, don't you?"

"Forget it," said the killer.

"You can't go to the law either," Parker told him. He looked past the killer, over at the woman. "I've got to force the names out of him," he said. "I don't like that kind of job. You want to try it? I'll tie him. And gag his mouth so he can't holler."

She smiled again, leaned far over the edge of the bed, and looked down at the killer.

"Yes," she said. "I've never done anything like that. I'd like to try." Her tongue peeked out past her lips. She moistened her lips, and looked down, and smiled.

Parker was pleased. He'd figured her right, every step of the way. He hadn't figured the unloading yet, but that would come when necessary. When it was time to get rid of her, split with her, he'd find the way. Not kill her, just unload her.

He looked down to see if he'd figured the killer right, too. He had. The killer was staring up at the smiling face of the woman, balloonlike, in the air above him. His pale eyes seemed larger, and the sweat had started on his face again. His fingers were clenching and unclenching and his cheeks seemed hollower, thinner.

Parker said, "What's your name?"

"Go to hell," said the killer. But his voice was higher and thinner and not completely under control.

Parker got to his feet. "We'll use two of my ties," he said. "You. Get into the chair."

The killer didn't move.

Parker stepped on his ankle. The killer gasped, and Parker stepped off the ankle again and said, "Get into the chair."

The woman said, "Tell him to take his pants off."

The killer closed his eyes. His whole face seemed sunken now, more pallid. He said, "Clint Stern. That's my name, Clint Stern."

Parker saw the woman pouting. She leaned back against the pillow again and lit a cigarette. She wouldn't meet Parker's eye.

Parker asked, "Who fingered me?"

"Jake Menner."

"Who is he?"

"A collector. He collects from the books around the hotels."

"All right. Who gives you the assignments?"

"Jim St. Clair."

"In New York?"

"Yes."

"Where do I get in touch with him?"

Stern's eyes flickered and his brow creased with worry lines. "You're making me dead, man," he said.

Parker said to the woman, "Maybe you'll get a chance at him after all."

Stern said, "I'll be dead anyway. What's the difference?" He sounded bitter, as though an injustice had been done him.

"I'm not talking about dead," Parker told him. "She won't let you die. Will you, Bett?"

She shrugged. She no longer seemed very interested. She knew Stern was going to give in without her doing anything. So did Parker. So did Stern. He said, "He runs a club in Brooklyn. On Kings Highway, near Utica Avenue."

"What's it called?"

"The Three Kings." Stern closed his eyes again. Every time he closed them, he looked like a corpse. He said, "You're killing me, man." He sounded tired, that was all.

"This guy Menner," said Parker. "You were supposed to call him when the job was done. Right?"

"Yes," said Stern.

Parker pointed. "There's the phone. Call him."

Stern sat up. Then he winced and put his hand to his bruised temple. He winced again, away from the hand, and looked bleakly at the spot of blood that had come off on his palm. "Maybe I got a concussion," he said.

"Move faster," said Parker.

Stern got to his feet, climbing up the chair. He moved as though he were dizzy. He stumbled when he moved away from the chair, and almost fell down. He made it to the writing desk where the phone was, and leaned against the wall. He picked up the receiver as though it was heavy, and started to dial. Then he looked over at Parker and said, "What do I say?"

"Parker's dead."

Stern finished dialing, and lifted the receiver to his ear. He waited, dull-eyed. From the middle of the room Parker heard the click and the metallic chatter when the phone was answered at the other end.

Stern said, "This is Stern. Let me talk to Menner."

There was a brief metallic chatter again, then silence. Stern leaned against the wall. Perspiration was streaming down his face, and his eyes looked heavier and heavier.

Finally, the phone chattered again, rousing him. He said, "Menner?" His eyes got brighter, feverish. He licked his lips. A kind of sick nervousness seemed to be pumping through him.

Parker watched him, and knew he was getting ready to tell

Menner the truth. He whispered, "Remember the woman, Stern."

Stern slumped. He said, "It's done. He's dead." Questioning sounds. "No. No trouble." His voice was as flat and lifeless as his eyes. "Yes. All right. Good-by."

But he remained leaning against the wall, head bowed, phone to his ear. Parker went over and took the phone away from him and hung it up. He said, "Where did you just call?"

"Floral Court. Rampon Boulevard."

"What number?"

"Twelve. Twelve Floral Court."

"How many others there?"

"Five or six. It's a poker game."

"All right. You got any money? Stern! You got any money?"

"Not on me."

"Where you can get it."

"Yes." He was acting as though he'd been doped.

"You better get it and take off. South—out of the country."

"Yes."

"It won't do any good to try again. It won't work. And it wouldn't mean anything to the Outfit anyway. They're going to know you missed the first time, so they'll know they can't count on you."

"Yes."

"Take off," Parker told him.

Stern stepped away from the wall, and stopped. His eyes

swiveled up in their sockets and he fell over on his face, loose and limp.

Parker shook his head, irritated. He said to Bett, "Wait here." He pulled a pair of pants on, grabbed Stern under the shoulders, and dragged him to the floor. He pulled the door open and looked outside. It was a quarter to four in the morning, and the hall was empty. Parker dragged Stern down to the end of the hall and opened the door to the interior fire stairs. He pulled Stern through and shut the door again. A dim bulb faintly illuminated each metal landing up and down the stairwell.

Parker propped Stern up in the corner and checked his pulse. He was still alive, but not by much. When he'd fallen, he'd hit the bruised place on his temple. It was bleeding a little bit again.

"Die some place else," Parker told him. He pinched him, and jabbed him in the ribs, then snapped his finger sharply against the underpart of Stern's nose. Stern came out of it groggily. His eyes were unfocused, and if Parker had asked him his name he wouldn't have known the answer. Or what the date was, or what city he was in, or where he'd been born. But he could understand simple orders, and he could make his body move.

Keeping his voice low, Parker said, "Get on your feet."

Stern tried, but he couldn't do it alone. Parker helped him get upright. When he was up, he could stay up, one hand pressed against the wall. His head was down, chin sunk in his chest, but his eyes were half-opened. He could still hear.

Parker said, "When I go out this door, go down those steps there. Do you hear me? When I go out this door, go down those steps there."

Stern nodded minutely.

Satisfied, Parker stepped back and opened the door. He stood in the doorway and watched Stern take the first step toward the descending metal stairs. He turned away, closed the door behind him, and walked back down the hall. Behind him, he could hear the muffled thumping as Stern fell.

He went back to the room and it was empty. He frowned, looked around, and saw the .32 was gone but the .25 was still there. He stood looking at the place where the .32 had been and wondered what she wanted from him that would require blackmail.

But he didn't have time to waste on her now. When she came back, he'd decide what to do.

He locked the door and dressed hurriedly. The .25 with the silencer made an awkward, bulky package inside his coat.

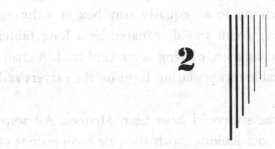

2

In the center of the *U* was a dry concrete fountain, littered with papers. The three sides of the *U* were Floral Court; latticework supported tired vines and separated the court from Rampon Boulevard. By day, Floral Court was pink stucco with green doors, but at four in the morning, it was black, with one square of yellow light spilling out, framing the dry fountain.

No air-conditioners here. The windows were open, and breathing sounds of sleepers mingled in the middle of the *U*, punctuated by the flat clatter of chips from the yellow window at the back.

Parker came silently through the opening in the latticework and stopped to take the awkward .25 from under his coat. The .32 would have been better. He cursed Bett, and moved again, close to the stucco wall, passing the open windows from which came the sounds of breathing.

The door marked 12 was just to the left of the lighted window. Parker passed it and crouched to peer over the window sill. Inside there was a tiny box of a living room with a wide archway to an equally tiny box of a dining room. The dining room was dominated by a long table, around which sat six men, playing seven card stud. A chandelier over the table threw glaring light on the players and the cards.

Any one of the six could have been Menner. All were stocky, fortyish, sour-looking, with the pale complexions of permanent Florida residents. They spoke only to announce their bets, not calling one another by name.

Parker considered. He had to get inside. The window was no good; too much light spilled onto it, and two of the players sat facing it. He straightened, moved to the side, and cautiously tried the door. As he'd expected, it was locked. So he'd have to take a chance on the back. He moved away from the building, retraced his steps around the *U* to the latticework, then stepped out to the sidewalk.

Rampon Boulevard was deserted. It was lined on both sides with stucco *U*'s, all of them resembling Floral Court. Parker turned left and walked down to the corner, counting courts. Floral was fourth from the corner. Parker went down the side street and turned at the driveway which ran behind the courts and was separated from them by rows of garages. The darkness back there was almost complete; with only a sliver of moon in the sky.

He went between two garages and came to the rear of Floral Court. By daylight, the pink stucco was crumbling and fading, the rear doors were grimed with age, the little patch of ground between court and garage was weed-pocked dirt. By night, the area was a black emptiness.

No light from number 12 leaked out to the back. Parker had to go by sound; he could hear the faint clicking of the chips. He found the rear door and the rear window; both were locked. But the wood of the doorframe was rotten; Parker leaned his weight against the door and felt it give. If he didn't have to worry about noise, he could go through the door in two seconds.

He had a pocketknife. He took it out, opened it, and forced the blade between door and frame till he found the lock. Then he pulled on the knob, pulling the door away from the frame, gouging the knife into the soft wood around the lock bolt. The wood made small cracking sounds, but it gave. He forced the blade under it and the bolt was free. Parker pushed gently, and the door opened. He stepped through and pushed the door closed behind him.

He was in a miniature kitchen. An open door on the right led to a bedroom, which he could barely see. Ahead, a yellow crack outlined a swing door that led to a short hallway. Through the crack, he could see that the hallway was flanked by the bathroom on one side and a second bedroom on the other. The dining room was straight ahead.

Parker pushed the swing door open slowly, till he could peer through at the dining room. Only one of the players was in sight, the one at the head of the table. He was concentrating his full attention on the cards. Parker slipped through the doorway, getting the .25 into his hands again, and strode quickly to the dining room. He stood in the entrance and said, "Freeze."

Six faces spun to gape at him. He let them see the gun, and said, "Face front. Look at your cards. Quick!"

They did as they were told. One of them, looking down at his cards, said, "You're making a mistake, fella. You don't want to knock over this game."

Parker said, "Menner, collect the wallets."

One of the six looked up. So that was Menner. He stared at Parker, and suddenly recognition struck him and left him ashen-faced. He sat gaping.

"Fast, Menner," Parker prodded him.

One of the others muttered, "How come he knows you, Jake?"

"Shut up. I'm waiting, Menner."

Menner held his hands out in front of his face and shook them, as though clearing away cobwebs. "Stern," he said. "Stern."

"You'll see him in a few minutes. Collect the wallets. The rest of you, keep your hands on the table, your eyes on the cards. Menner, you reach into their pockets for the wallets. You don't want to bring out anything but wallets."

The man who'd spoken before said, "Do like he says, Jake. We'll take care of him later. We don't want any trouble here."

Menner obediently got to his feet. He went around the table, reaching into the other players' pockets, bringing out

the wallets. Parker told him, "Put them in your coat pockets.
Your own wallet, too. And the bills from the table."

"Listen," said Menner. His voice was shaky. "Listen, you
don't under——"

"Shut up."

Menner had all the wallets in his coat pockets. He looked
baggier than before, and forlorn, like a half-deflated balloon.
He stood waiting for Parker to tell him what to do next.

Parker said, "Tell them why I'm here."

"Listen, honest to Christ, it ain't the way——"

"Tell them why I'm here."

The player who did all the talking said, "Do what he says,
Jake. I'd like to hear it myself."

"They—they sent down this gun from New York, for this
guy here, this Parker. They said I was to—I was to finger the
job. That's all it was, I swear to Christ."

"The rest of it," said Parker.

"That's all! What else, for Christ's sake?"

"You fingered me in the first place. That's why the gun
came down."

The player said, "That's between you and Jake, buddy.
Don't take it out on us."

"It's all the same Outfit. Give me your coat, Menner."

"For Christ's sake, Parker, I—"

"Give me your coat."

Stuttering, Menner took the coat off. Parker reached out
for it, waiting for Menner to try flipping it in his face but

Menner was cowed. He handed it over without causing trouble, and stepped back to take his medicine.

Because it was such a light, untrustworthy gun, Parker pulled the trigger three times. He turned and went out the back way, clearing the back door before Menner hit the carpet or the other five could get out of their chairs.

3

Parker sat at the writing desk fumbling with pen and paper, frowning. He wasn't used to writing letters:

FRANK,
   The Outfit thinks it has a greevance on me. It doesn't. But it keeps sending its punks around to make trouble. I told their headman I'd give them money trouble if they didn't quit, and they didn't quit. You told me one time about a lay you worked out for that gambling place outside Boston, and you'd do me a favor if you knocked it off in the next couple weeks. I'm writing some of the other boys, too, so you can be sure they'll be too busy to go looking for you special. I don't want a cut and I can't come in on the job because I'll be busy making trouble myself. You can always get in touch with me care of Joe Sheer out in Omaha. Maybe we'll work together again some day.
                                                                    PARKER

It took three drafts to get it down the way he wanted it. He read the final version through, decided it was all right, and nodded to himself. Only one thing bothered him. He went over to the telephone, dialed the operator, and asked her to spell "grievance" for him, because he wasn't sure he had it right. She checked with someone else, gave him the correct spelling, and he copied the letter over again.

He then went on to the other letters. They were easier, because he just copied the first one word for word, except for the particular job he wanted each man to do. In some cases, there was no particular job, so he wrote instead: "Maybe you know some Outfit operation that would be an easy lay, and if you do you can do me a favor and knock it off in the next couple weeks."

He completed six letters, and then looked out the windows and saw it was daytime. The dry fountain looked like a remnant from a lost civilization. It was not quite seven o'clock, and he was back in 12 Floral Court, again. If the other poker players were anxious to get their money and wallets back, they might be able to check back through Menner's friends or other people in the Outfit and find out where Parker was supposed to be staying, so it would be a good idea to stay away from the hotel for a while. But none of them would be in any hurry to come back to Floral Court. There was a body in the bedroom closet.

Parker had run as far as the backyard; then he had turned to the left and run a distance of three courts. Behind him, he'd heard the poker players emerge. One of them had a flashlight, and all of them boiled out past the garages. He waited, and after a while they came back and went into the apartment. He kept waiting until he heard three cars start up out front on Rampon Boulevard. Then he went back in. The lights were off, the place was empty, and Menner was in the bedroom closet. The poker players would be running around establishing alibis.

In the sideboard in the dining room, he found stationery and envelopes. He pulled the shade down in the living room, sat at the dining-room table, and started writing letters. After six of them, he went over to the window, pulled the shade away, looked out at the decaying fountain, and decided he'd waited long enough. He went back to the table and wrote one more letter:

BETT,

You took the gun. You want something from me and then you'll give me the gun back. I don't have time now to fool with you. I got to take care of the problem that put that Stern on my back. I'll get in touch with you within a month. If you don't hear from me, turn the gun over to the law. I guess there's skin scrapings from Stern on it or something to tie me in with what happened to Stern, and it'll keep.

PARKER

He looked at it, then crossed out "Parker," and wrote in its place, "Chuck." He put the note in an envelope, wrote her name on the outside, and tucked the envelope in his pocket. The other six letters went into the same pocket. He got the .25, stripped the silencer off it, and went to the bedroom closet. He pulled Menner out onto the bedroom floor, wiped his own prints from the gun, and closed Menner's hand around it. It might not hold up as suicide—the angle was probably wrong, and Menner had two too many bullets in him—but it should help to slow the law down. And the gun, if it could be traced at all, couldn't be traced past Stern to Parker.

Out back, he threw the silencer into a garbage can. Then he walked around to Rampon Boulevard and caught a cab. "Hotel Maharajah."

There was no one he recognized in the lobby. He left the note for Bett at the desk and went up to his room. It was empty. As far as he could tell, no one had been in it. He packed his suitcase, stuffing the six wallets into it, with the identity cards and driver's licenses, but without the seventeen hundred dollars they'd once contained, and went downstairs to check out. This time, he was going to settle things with the Outfit once and for all. This time, he was going straight to Bronson.

4

Last year, it was. Parker had let his finances run low, and a job that had seemed promising had fallen through in the planning stage, so when this Mal Resnick told him about the island job he decided to take it on. Munitions were being sold by a private group of Americans and Canadians to a lunatic group of South American *fidelistas,* and a tiny Pacific island had been chosen for the transfer of arms and money. This particular island had been picked because it was uninhabited and because the Seabee-built World War II airfield there was still usable. Mal and Parker and the others decided to take the money away.

There were six of them in it: a Canadian named Chester, who'd originally found out about the deal; a man named Ryan, who knew how to fly a plane; a methodical, reliable gunman named Sill; Parker's wife, Lynn; Mal Resnick and Parker. With Lynn waiting in the abandoned house they'd chosen as their California base, the five men had flown to the island, turned the trick with a minimum of fuss, and flown back to the mainland. And that night, in the California house, the double-crossing had started.

Mal had begun by talking to Ryan, telling him Parker was planning a cross. Then he'd killed Chester in his sleep, and had gone to Ryan to tell him Parker had started, had already done for Chester, and that Sill was siding with Parker. Ryan wasn't a subtle man; he accepted the story the way Mal fed it to him. Later it was Ryan who finished Sill.

Then Parker's wife, Lynn, had been brought into it. Mal had wanted her from the first minute he'd seen her. He now saw a way to get her. He used the threat of death to force her to kill Parker herself, and she did her best. But her first bullet slammed into Parker's belt buckle and he dropped; and she emptied the gun over his head.

So far as Mal knew, the operation was still sweet. He put a torch to the house, shot Ryan in the back, and took off with Lynn and the ninety-thousand-dollar haul. He had a purpose for that money. Four years before, he'd worked in Chicago for the Outfit, but he'd loused up, dumping forty thousand dollars of uncut snow when he mistook the Outfit tail for a plainclothesman. The Outfit had let him live, which had surprised him, but had told him not to come back without the cash to pay for his mistake. Now Mal had the cash.

He took Lynn with him. She was now a silent block of ice, but he thought he could eventually thaw her out. They went to New York, and he gave the Outfit back every penny—with interest and penalties—a little over fifty thousand. He invested the rest, and sat around waiting for the Outfit to offer him something. He got a job, a better one than he'd had before, and settled in New York to live the way he thought he should.

But Parker wasn't dead. Badly bruised by the bullet that had slammed his belt buckle into his stomach, he'd managed to crawl out of the burning house wearing nothing but a pair of trousers and had wandered, half-delirious, three days before being picked up. He had no identification on him and no money. He refused to tell the law anything, and wound up with a six-month vag stint on a prison farm—his one and only fall. It also caused him to lose some of his anonymity— his fingerprints went on file, under the name he'd grudgingly given them: Ronald Kasper. Even when he'd been in the Army—'42 to '44, when he got his BCD for black-marketeering—he'd managed to avoid having his fingerprints recorded by bribing a file clerk to replace them with his own. So now he had one more reason to get hold of Mal.

Finally, he broke out of the prison farm, bummed his way across the country, and went to New York to look for Mal and Lynn. They were separated now, Mal having given up trying to get Lynn to respond to him. Parker found Lynn—and she killed herself. He couldn't have finished her off, but she did it herself. Then he found Mal, and evened the account.

So Lynn and Mal were both dead, but Parker was still broke. Mal had given his share—forty-five thousand—to the Outfit, so Parker went to the Outfit to get it back. They hadn't wanted to give it to him, so he used pressure, disrupting the New York organization, and threatening to cause them trouble all across the country if he didn't get his money.

"I've worked my particular line for eighteen years," he told them. "In that time, I've worked with about a hundred different men. Among them, they've worked with just about every pro in the business. There's you people with your organization, and there's us. We don't have any organization, but we're professionals. We know each other. We stick with each other. And we don't hit the syndicate. We don't hit casinos, or lay-off bookies, or narcotic caches. You're sitting there wide open, you can't squeal to the law, but we don't hit you.

"If you don't give me my money, I write letters, to those hundred men I told you about. I tell them: 'the syndicate hit me for forty-five G. Do me a favor and hit them back once, when you've got the chance.'

"Maybe half of them will say the hell with it. The other half are like me—they've got a job all cased. A lot of us are like that. You organized people are so wide open. We walk into a syndicate place and we look around, and just automatically we think it over, we think about it like a job. We don't do anything about it, because you people are on the same side as us, but we think about it. I've walked around for years with three syndicate grabs all mapped out in my head, but I've never done anything about it. The same with a lot of the people I know. So all of a sudden they've got the green light, they've got an excuse. They'll grab for it."

They weren't sure whether it was bluff or not, but they

agreed to pay. Parker was causing them too much trouble anyway. He'd killed Carter, one of the two men in charge of the New York area, and then managed to get a gun on the surviving boss, Fairfax. With Parker standing over him, Fairfax telephoned Bronson, head of the national organization, and Bronson came to terms. He put the forty-five thousand in a trap, and Parker walked through the trap and came out on the other side with the money. Knowing that the Outfit—and Bronson personally—would now try to hunt him down and kill him, Parker had gone to a plastic surgeon who worked outside the law, and came out with a new face.

But now the Outfit knew about the new face. And they also knew about his cover name, Willis.

It was time to bring it to an end, time to write the letters, and time to talk to Bronson. He was somewhere in the country. Parker would find him, and make an end to it.

Two

1

The woman with orange hair sat on the porch and watched Parker come walking down the rutted road toward the house. This was in the middle of the Georgia scrub country, west of Cordele, about thirty miles north of Albany. The land was brown and dry; the ruts in the road rock-hard. The house was gray frame, two stories high, a narrow, tall, rectangular box in the middle of a dead land, with blind uncurtained windows and an afterthought of a porch stuck askew on the front. A barn stood back of the house to one side; there was a long garage on the other side. Rusting automobile parts were scattered on the baked clay between house and garage. A lone dead tree stood gray and naked in front of the house with a rusty pulley arrangement fixed to a thick lower branch. Except for the woman with orange hair, the place looked deserted.

Yesterday, after checking out of the hotel, Parker had taken a plane to Atlanta, and then doubled back, taking a bus south to Macon, and another bus further south to Cordele. A bus headed for Columbus had taken him west of Cordele along an empty black-top road to the twin-rut turnoff, and carrying his suitcase, he'd walked the three miles in to the house.

It was November, but the land was still dry and the air was hot. After three miles, the suitcase got heavy. The rutted road made walking difficult. It would have been easier if he'd left the suitcase in Cordele, but he didn't want to go through there again.

As he walked past the dead tree with the pulley on it, a lean mongrel rose up on the porch next to the chair the woman was sitting in. The hound stretched and yawned, then looked up at the woman and looked out at Parker. He watched Parker and waited, not barking or moving or doing anything.

Parker stopped where he was and dropped the suitcase onto the ground. He said, "Chemy around?"

The woman asked, "Who wants him?"

"Parker."

"Parker, you say?"

"Parker."

She lifted her head and called, "Elly!"

A boy of about fourteen, as lean and silent as the dog, came out of the house and stood there. The woman said to him, "Go on over to the garage, see if Chemy ain't there. Fella name of Parker lookin' for him."

Parker said, "Tell him I got a new face."

The boy turned his head and gazed at him, the same way the dog gazed. The woman frowned and said, "What the hell kind of talk is that?" She was very fat, forty or forty-five, with a fat white face under the orange hair. She was wearing a dark-blue dress with pink flowers on it.

"Plastic surgery," Parker told her. "He'll have to recognize me by voice and build and what I know."

The woman shook her head. "Go on, Elly," she said. To Parker she said, "You can wait right there."

The boy came down off the porch and walked around to the garage. He was wearing dungarees and nothing else. He was tanned as dark as an Indian, and his sun-faded blond hair was shaggy and long. He opened a door in the side of the garage and went inside, closing the door after him. The door squealed loudly in the silence, and seemed to affect the light oddly. Instead of a shaft of sunlight angling through the opening and lighting the interior of the garage, it was as though a shaft of darkness pooled out on the ground outside the door when it was opened.

Parker asked, "You want a cigarette?"

"Thank you, no."

"I think I'll have one," he said.

He had wanted her to know what he was reaching for. She nodded, and he slowly took cigarettes and matches from his pocket. Then he stood smoking in the hot, dry air. The dog watched him, unwinking.

The squealing door opened again, and the boy stood in the

pool of darkness, gazing at him. Then he turned and said something to somebody inside. Parker waited.

The boy came into the sunlight again, and a short, skinny man in overalls came out after him. The man had dry black hair and a narrow face. His bare shoulders were pale and covered with freckles. He came walking over and stood studying Parker for a minute.

Then he said, "Well, I'll be darned. Got yourself a new face, eh?"

"It's your brother I wanted," Parker told him.

The skinny man frowned. "What's that you say?"

"I asked for your brother."

"The hell," said the skinny man. "You asked for Chemy."

"And you're Kent."

"What makes you think so?"

"Go tell your brother I want to buy a car. Like the Ford with the bullet holes in the trunk."

The skinny man scratched his head. "You sound like Parker," he said. "You sure as hell act like Parker. And you know the right stuff to *be* Parker. But you don't look like Parker."

"Plastic surgery. I told your wife."

"Lemme see if Chemy's here."

"I'll come along. It's hot out in the sun."

The skinny man frowned and said, "You got all Parker's brass, I'll give you that much. What would you do if that dog there took to leap at you?"

Parker glanced at the dog. "Break its neck," he said.

"Yuh. And what if I was to whip out a pistol and start shooting down on you?"

"I'd take it away like Handy McKay did that time."

The skinny man flushed, and on the porch the woman started to laugh. She had a high Betty Boop sort of giggle, completely different from her speaking voice. The skinny man turned to her and said, "Shut your face!" She stopped immediately. He spun back to Parker. "I think you're a phony, mister," he said. "I think you better get off this property."

Parker shook his head. Over the skinny man's head, he called to the woman, "You want to keep that dog right there next to you." Then he started walking toward the garage. The skinny man hollered and made as if to come after him, but then he stopped. The woman rested her hand on the dog's head and watched Parker cross the yard.

The side door of the garage opened again, and a man came out with a shotgun cradled on his arm. He was short and skinny, like the other one, with the same kind of narrow face and dead hair. He was similarly dressed in faded blue, bibbed overalls. They were obviously brothers, but what was petulance in Kent's face became strength in Chemy's. He came out, closed the door after him, and said, "Stop right there, friend."

Parker stopped. "Hello, Chemy," he said.

Chemy looked past him at Kent. "Well? Is he Parker or ain't he Parker?"

Kent didn't answer at first. Parker half-turned and looked back at him. "Am I, Kent?"

"Yuh," said Kent. He said it reluctantly, and glared at the woman, as though daring her to laugh again. But she was silent, her face carefully blank as she watched them, her fingers scratching the top of the dog's head between its ears.

To his brother, Chemy said, "Get us a drink. Come on in, Parker." He led the way back into the garage, and set the shotgun against the wall beside the door.

The garage was big enough to hold four cars. At the moment, there was a fifteen-year-old red Ford pickup truck parked down by the far wall, and an orange Volkswagen next to it. The Volkswagen's rear lid was open and the engine had been removed and was lying on two-by-fours behind the car. The back seat had been taken out, too, and was leaning against the side of the pickup truck. All along the back wall was a workbench, littered with tools, small parts, lengths of wire, and pieces of metal. Automobile body parts were stacked here and there in the remaining space, and two engines hung by chain and pulley from the roof beams. A small plastic radio on the workbench was blaring country and western music; a girl singer with a twang as bad as a harelip was singing about unrequited love.

"Well, now," said Chemy. "You sure changed your face around. But you're still just as mean as ever."

"That brother of yours needs a talking to."

Chemy shrugged, and grinned faintly. "If you were Parker, you'd do what you done. If you weren't, you'd let him chase you off the place."

Parker shrugged. It didn't matter one way or the other. He was just hot from the walk.

Chemy said, "Take a look down here at this VW. What do you think of this? A '57 Ford straight-six engine in there in back, and re-did Chevy brakes. Think she'll move?"

Parker frowned at the Volkswagen. "No," he said.

"No? Why in hell not?"

"Where's your cooling system?"

"Right where the back seat used to be, with scoops down through the floor. '51 Plymouth radiator assembly that fits real nice."

Parker knew he was supposed to think of every objection he could, so Chemy could show him how smart he was. He said, "Not enough weight for the power. She'll go like a motorboat, with her nose up in the air. You'd have to take corners at ten miles an hour."

"No, sir. I've weighted down that front end, so your center of gravity is right *here*." He touched a spot low on the side, just behind the door.

"That's pretty far back."

"Oh, she'll jounce, I know she will. But the weight is just far enough up so you can take corners just about any damn speed you like."

Parker shook his head. "She'll jounce apart," he said. "She won't last a year."

"I know damn well she won't. But she'll last a month, and that's all she's wanted for. A car that looks slow but goes like a bat out of hell. That's what this girl is. A special order."

"So everything's worked out then."

"No, it ain't." Chemy frowned at the car. "One damn thing—you know what that is?"

"What?"

"I can't make her *sound* like a VW. I've tried all sorts of mufflers; I've run pipe back and forth underneath there till she looked like a plate of spaghetti; but she never does sound like a VW. You know that little 'cough-cough' sound the VW's got? Your VW fires slow, is what it is, and I be damned if I can get the effect." He glared at the car again, shaking his head. "I'll get it," he said.

"Sure." Parker knew he would. Chemy made cars do whatever he wanted them to do.

"Sure," agreed Chemy. He turned away from the Volkswagen. "So what do you want? A car? Anything special?"

"Just a car. With clean papers."

"How clean? To sell?"

"No. To show if I'm stopped for speeding."

"Takin' her out of the state?"

"Up north."

"All right then."

The garage door opened and Kent came in, carrying three glasses and a bottle of corn liquor as colorless as water. He glanced sullenly at his brother and Parker, then went over to the workbench, set the glasses down, and poured three drinks.

Chemy and Parker went over and they all drank. It was good liquor, leaving a harsh wood-smoke taste on the tongue and a bright burning at the back of the throat.

Chemy set his glass down and cleared his throat. "How new?" he asked.

"Doesn't matter. But I'll be going maybe a couple thousand miles in it, so I don't want one ready to fall apart."

Chemy nodded. "When?"

"Now."

"Always in a hurry." Chemy grinned at his brother. "This Parker," he said. "Always in a hurry, huh?"

"Huh," said Kent. He was being surly, staring into his empty glass.

Chemy winked at Parker, finished his own drink, and said, "I got two in the barn right now, but not what you got to have. Both hot, both no good. I got to take a ride. How much you want to pay?"

"I'll go a thousand—if I have to."

"Well, maybe you won't have to. You go set on the porch a while. Come on, Kent."

They went outside and Parker strolled over to the house while the two brothers went around behind the garage. He went up on the porch and sat on the other chair. The woman grinned at him, showing spaces where she'd lost teeth, and said, "I guess I must of heard about you."

"Maybe," said Parker.

A six-year-old Pontiac station wagon with Chemy at the wheel and his brother beside him appeared from behind the garage and went off down the rutted road. Parker sat and smoked, waiting. The woman tried to start a conversation with him once or twice, but he didn't encourage her, so she quit. The dog got up again after a while, went down off the porch, and loped away around the house. A while later Parker got to his feet, went into the house, and walked through rooms of sagging furniture to the kitchen, where he got himself a drink of water. He didn't see the boy. The woman followed him in, and stood in the kitchen doorway, smiling hesitantly at him, but not saying anything. When he started out of the kitchen, she murmured, "We got time."

He shook his head, and went back out on the porch. She stayed inside the house.

He waited three hours, and the sun was turning red way off near the western horizon when Chemy and Kent came back. Kent was driving the Pontiac this time, and Chemy was following him in a four-year-old blue Oldsmobile with Alabama plates. Kent took the Pontiac around behind the garage, and Chemy stopped the Oldsmobile in front of the house. He got out and patted the hood and said, "Well? What do *you* think?"

Chemy grinned, shrugging his shoulders. "I don't know yet. I figure maybe. The car's hot in Florida, and the plates are hot in Alabama, but the plates are off a LaSalle, so you got nothing to worry about."

"LaSalle? There's still some of them around?"

"Give me three days around here, Parker, I'll find you a Marmon."

"I don't want a Marmon."

"Sure not. I'll check this out for you. She run good coming in."

Kent had come around from behind the garage, and was now opening one set of doors in front. Chemy got back into the Oldsmobile and drove it into the garage, next to the Volkswagen. Parker walked over after him, went inside, and Kent followed, closing the doors.

The two brothers spent half an hour checking the car, mostly in silence. Every once in a while, Kent would say, "Look at this," and Chemy would bend close and peer, and then say, "It's okay." A few times it wasn't okay, and the two would work to make it okay.

Finally Chemy said, "She's better than I thought. A southern car all the way, Parker, got none of your northern corrosion."

"I thought it was from Florida. What about salt corrosion?"

"*Stolen* from Florida. She used to have Tennessee plates on her."

"What about papers?"

"Right here. Just fill in whatever name you like."

Parker had a driver's license in his wallet, from one of the poker players who'd been with Menner. It had the name Maurice Kebbler on it, so that was the name he wrote on the registration. Then he said, "Wait a minute," and went out to the suitcase still lying on the ground in front of the house. He picked it up and carried it back to the garage. The woman with orange hair was on the porch again, standing there, watching Parker with no expression on her face.

Parker went into the garage and opened the suitcase on the

workbench. There was an envelope in the side pocket of the suitcase, and he took it out and slid seven hundred-dollar bills from it and put them on the bench. Then he put the envelope back in the pocket and closed the suitcase.

Chemy watched the whole operation, and nodded. "Good enough," he said. "Kent, open them doors."

Kent opened the doors, and the woman with orange hair was standing there. Her face was flushed now, and she looked upset. She said, "Kent, that bastard raped me."

Kent just stared at her. Chemy frowned at her and said, "Don't be foolish."

"Godamit, I say he raped me!"

Kent turned, looking shaken. "Parker. What the hell is this?"

Parker shrugged.

Chemy said to the woman, "Come off it, will you?"

Kent shook his head, looking goggle-eyed at his brother. "Why would she say it, Chemy? If he didn't do nothing, why would she say he did?"

"Ask Parker if you want. Don't ask me."

Parker said, "She made me the offer and I turned her down."

Kent looked ashen. "You're a lying son a bitch!" he shouted. He reached out, got a wrench in his hand, and started across the garage toward Parker.

The woman turned her head and screamed. "Judge! Here, you, Judge!" And whistled shrilly through the gaps between her teeth.

"Leave the dog out of this!" shouted Chemy.

"Don't do anything stupid, Kent," Parker said.

"I'll break your head open, you son of a bitch." Kent was as white as the inside of a potato, and he shuffled slowly forward, the wrench held out from his body in his right hand.

Parker turned his head, saying, "Chemy, you want me to kill your brother?"

"No, I don't think so."

"Then call him off."

"I couldn't do that, Parker. I'm sorry, but I couldn't do that."

Parker frowned. "Chemy, do you believe that bag?"

"That ain't for me to say, Parker; I ain't the husband. I'm just the brother-in-law."

"Then you'll keep out, won't you?"

"Unless my brother gets hurt."

Kent said, "I won't be the one gets hurt." He dashed in suddenly, face contorted, arm looping up and over with the wrench.

Parker ran inside the descending curve, butting Kent in the face with the top of his head, kneeing him, chopping upward with the right side of his hand against the soft underpart of Kent's upper arm. Kent cried out as his arm went dead and the wrench fell to the floor. Parker stepped back and hit him twice, and Kent followed the wrench down and didn't move.

The woman was screaming for the dog again. Chemy wasn't saying anything at all now, but was leaning against the side of the Oldsmobile and looking on with an expression of regret on his face.

Parker turned and strode swiftly to the side door. He grabbed up the shotgun and turned with it as the dog, lean and fast and silent, came loping on a long curve into the garage. The woman was screaming "Sic 'im," and Chemy was shouting for the dog to come back. But the woman's voice was louder and the dog kept coming. Parker had the shotgun by the barrels and he swung it like a baseball bat. The dog leaped into the swing. The wooden stock cracked against the side of its head and sent it tumbling away to the side, to crash into a pile of junk and lay still.

Parker turned the shotgun around and said, "My best move is to finish the three of you."

"I'm neutral, Parker," Chemy said.

"No, you're not. That bag wants to see your brother get killed, Chemy. She sent him after me hoping I'd do it."

The woman stared at him, openmouthed.

"Shut up," said Chemy. "Parker never touched you."

Parker said, "Can you convince your brother?"

"Sure I can. Why should I?"

"I don't leave loose ends behind me."

Chemy thought it over, gazing down at his brother, unconscious on the floor. Finally, he said, "I guess I see what you mean. All right, I'll convince him."

"How?"

Chemy grinned bleakly. "She offered it to me, too, once or twice."

"Lies!"

They both ignored her. Parker said, "I'll wake him up."

"No. You take off. It'd be better if we was alone when I told him. He'd be able to take it better."

"You *are* going to tell him?"

"I swear it, Parker."

"All right." Parker put the shotgun down.

Chemy asked, "You want to give this bitch a ride into town? I figure she ought to be outa here before Kent gets the word."

"She can walk." ·

"I guess she can at that." He turned and looked at the woman. "Get started," he said. "If Kent wants to kill you, I won't do nothing to stop him."

"You *took* the offer, you bastard!" she screamed at him.

Chemy turned his back on her, saying to Parker, "You might as well take off now. Sorry we had all this fuss."

"I'll be seeing you."

Parker stowed his suitcase on the back seat of the car. The woman, after hesitating a minute, had gone away from the garage, headed for the house. Parker backed the Oldsmobile out into the late sunlight, turned it around, saw the flash of orange hair in the living room window, and drove away down the rutted road, easing the car slowly and carefully across the bumps and potholes. When he got to the black-top road, he headed north. The Olds responded well. The upholstery was in rotten shape, the floor mats were chewed to pieces, and the paint job was all scratched up, but the engine purred nicely and the Olds leaped forward when he pressed the accelerator. He lit a cigarette, shifted position till he was comfortable, and headed north out of Georgia.

2

The operator wanted ninety-five cents. Parker dropped the coins in; then the phone went dead for a while. A little rubber-bladed fan was whirring up near the top of the booth but not doing much good. Parker shoved the door open a little, and the fan stopped. He adjusted the door again until it was open a crack and the fan still worked. The phone started clicking with the sounds of falling relays, then stopped, and a repeated ringing took over.

The phone was answered on the fourth ring by a male voice.

Parker said, "I'm trying to get Arnie LaPointe."

"Speaking."

"This is Parker. I want you to give Handy McKay a message from me."

"I'm not sure I'll see him."

"If you do."

"Sure, if I do."

"If he's got nothing on, I'd like to meet him at Madge's in Scranton next Thursday."

"Who should he ask for?"

"Me. Parker."

"What time Thursday?"

"Next Thursday. Not this Thursday."

"I got that. What time?"

"Nine o'clock."

"Morning or night?"

"For Christ's sake. Night."

"If I see him, I'll tell him."

"Thanks."

He hung up, and the coins clattered deeper into the box. He left the booth and went out of the drugstore. He was on the outskirts of Indianapolis, far enough away from the center of the city for the drugstore to have a parking lot. The blue Olds was there, nosed against the stucco side of the building.

Parker had had the Olds four days now, and it worked fine. He slid behind the wheel and pulled out of the lot. He was farther north now and, though the sun was bright, the air was cold. He headed east, through Speedway out to Clermont, and between Clermont and Brownsburg he turned off on a small road where a faded sign announced, "Tourist Accommodations." The land was flat, but heavily forested, and he was practically on top of the house before he saw it. He pulled around to the side and parked.

It was a big house painted white some years ago. Bay windows protruded from its sides with no pattern, like growths. The porch was broad with narrow rococo pillars. Four rocking chairs stood empty on the porch. A second-floor curtain flicked and was still.

Parker got out of the Olds and walked around to the front and up on the porch. A small, bald man in white shirt and gray pants with dark-blue suspenders appeared at the screen door and squinted out at him. He had a pair of wire-framed spectacles pushed up on his forehead, but he didn't bother to lower them, just squinted.

The plastic surgery Parker had had done seemed like a good idea at the time, but it made for complications. Nobody knew him anymore. He stood outside the screen door and said, "I'm looking for a room."

"Sorry," said the bald man. "We're all full up right now."

Parker looked up. There was a light over the door in a complicated fixture supposed to look like a lantern. He said, "I see you got that fixed."

"I did what?"

"The last time I was here," Parker told him, "Eddie Hill got drunk and took off after that girl of his and shot that light all to hell. Remember?"

Now the bald man did lower his glasses to his nose, and peered through them at Parker's face. "I don't remember you," he said.

"One time when Skimm was here," Parker said, "he buried

a wad of dough out back some place. If you haven't looked for it, you can now. He's dead."

"You know who you sound like?"

"Parker."

"Be damned if you don't."

A new voice, from inside the house, said, "Invite the gentleman in, Begley."

Begley pushed open the screen door. "Maybe you ought to come inside."

Parker went in and saw a man in the entrance to the parlor. He was holding a gun, but not aiming it anywhere in particular at the moment.

"Hi, Jacko," said Parker.

Jacko was chewing gum. He said, "You got the advantage on me, friend. I don't seem to recollect your name."

"Parker."

"Crap."

Begley had been leaning close, squinting up at Parker's face, and he now said, "No, now—wait a minute, Jacko. I be damned if it ain't Parker! He's had one of them face jobs, that's all."

"Oh, yeah?" Jacko frowned, chewing his gum. "Okay, who worked that Fort Wayne payroll job with you, back in '49?"

"You did."

"Sure. Just the two of us?"

"Bobby Gonzales drove. Joe Sheer worked the safe. The inside man was named Fahey or something like that. He tried to run out with the boodle and you took him up to Lake Michigan and threw him in."

"Where'd we hide out after the job?"

"In a trailer camp outside Goshen. It isn't there any more."

Parker turned to Begley. "Let's go sit down. I want to talk. You too, Jacko."

"I'm not satisfied yet," said Jacko.

"Then go to hell."

Jacko laughed. "Maybe you're Ronald Reagan with the FBI. How do I know?"

"You're scared of guns, Jacko, so you got no cartridge under the hammer. You'll have to pull that trigger twice before you get any action, and I can move faster than that. Put it away, or I'll take it away from you."

Begley laughed then, and said, "Nobody but Parker can irritate people so quick."

Jacko put the pistol inside his jacket, looking angry. "One of these days, Parker," he said, "I've got to check you out. Nobody's as mean as you talk."

"Maybe not." Parker went on past him into the parlor, where there was a sofa and three rocking chairs. He picked one of them, sat down, and said, "I want to talk anyway."

The other two came in and sat down. Begley said, "You want a room now?"

"No. Two weeks from now."

"You got something lined up?" Jacko asked him. "You want a hand, maybe?"

"No. I want to tell you a story." He told them quickly

about his trouble with the syndicate. Jacko sat impassive, chewing his gum. Begley listened, fascinated, blinking behind his spectacles.

"So I'm going to settle this thing with the Outfit once and for all," Parker finished. "That's why I'll need a room in a couple weeks."

"Why tell me?" asked Jacko.

"It's a chance for you. It's a chance for all the boys. The Outfit is full of cash, all untraceable, and they can't call in the law if they get taken. We've always left them alone, and they've always left us alone. Now they're making trouble for me. If you hit them, they'll blame me." He turned to Begley. "I want you to spread the word, anybody else drops in. Now's the time to hit the syndicate."

"For you?" demanded Jacko. "Why should I do anything for you, Parker?"

"Not for me. I don't want a cut or anything else. I'm just spreading the word. You know of any syndicate operation that would be an easy take?"

Jacko laughed. "Half a dozen," he said. "They pay the law and they figure that's all they got to do."

"So here's your chance, that's all."

"But it helps you, too, Parker."

"So what?"

Jacko shrugged. "I'll think it over."

Begley said, "I'll spread the word, Parker. You can count on me."

"Good."

"They should of paid you in the first place the way Bronson promised. It was your money."

Jacko said, "Maybe they didn't figure it that way."

"They figured it wrong," said Parker. He got to his feet. To Begley, he said, "I'll see you in a couple weeks."

"Okay." Begley walked him to the door. "Couple more boys you know upstairs. Want to say hello?"

"No time. Spread the word on the new face, too, will you?"

"Sure."

Parker went back out to the Olds. Begley stood on the porch staring after him as he drove away. He drove back to the highway and headed north again, crossing into Illinois, getting as far as Kankakee before stopping at a motel for the night. He wrote half a dozen more letters that night. This had been his routine all the way up from Georgia. Stop off to see one or two people every day along his route, and, at night, write letters to the men too far off the route for him to visit. He'd written about thirty letters so far, and seen seven people. If only a third of them took the chance he was suggesting, it would be enough. The Outfit would start to hurt.

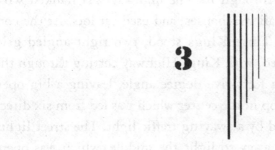

3

There was a large poster frame beside the entrance. In it, a faggot with black wavy hair smiled above his bow tie. His eyes were made up like Theda Bara's. Under the bow tie it said: RONNIE RANDALL & HIS PIANO—EVERY NITE! Over the entrance, small spots shone on huge silver letters against a black background: THE THREE KINGS. Pasted to the glass of the left-hand entrance door was the notice: *No cover, no minimum—except weekends.* Covering the glass of the other door was a poster: SALLY & THE SWINGERS—EVERY FRI. SAT. SUN! The building behind all this information was low and squat, made of concrete blocks painted a pale blue. Porthole windows marched away to the right of the entrance across the front of the building, showing amber bar lights deep inside, making it look like midnight in an aquarium. Parker drove by twice, very slowly, and then parked half a block away in the darkness of a side street.

This part of Brooklyn was a tight gridwork of two-story
row houses with Kings Highway gouging a broad black-top
diagonal down through it. The highway was flanked with
diners, bars, small warehouses, and used-car lots. At the corner where The Three Kings stood, two right-angled grid
streets intersected, with Kings Highway cutting through the
intersection at a forty-five degree angle, leaving a big open
space of black-top in the center which was fed from six directions and capped by a swaying traffic light. The street lights
were all too far away to light the middle, which was open,
bare, and black.

Eleven o'clock, Tuesday night. Darkness surrounded the
intersection everywhere except for the pool of light in front of
The Three Kings. Up and down Kings Highway were far
glimpses of other neon oases, but the grid tree-lined streets
were all shut up and dark.

Parker left the Olds in a slot with plenty of room in front,
so he could take off without backing and filling, and walked
to the intersection. November was ending, and Brooklyn was
cold with the wet bronchial cold of the harbor. Parker's breath
misted around him as he walked. He was wearing a topcoat,
but no hat, and he walked with his hands jammed deep into
his pockets. In one of his suit pockets was the gun he'd picked
up the day before in Wilmington, a short-barreled S & W .38
Special.

He was now ten days from Florida. Forty-seven letters had
been written; twelve men had been talked to personally. Four
of the twelve had said they'd been looking for an excuse like

this to hit the syndicate for years. Five more had said they'd
think it over, and three had copped out for one reason or another. Say a third would move out of the fifty-nine—twenty
jobs! Within a month, or less, the Outfit would be hit twenty
times, maybe more, all over the country.

Starting tonight.

Light washed down on Parker as he pushed open the door
and went into the club. Inside, amber light feebly silhouetted
the furnishings and customers. Two bartenders were blobs of
white behind the dark wooden bar, but tonight one of them
was unnecessary. Four women and three men were spaced
along the bar, and the booths on the other side of the room
were all empty. In back, twenty tables or so were arranged in
a semi-circle around a small platform, and on the platform
Ronnie Randall, twenty years older than his picture and very
tired, noodled at the piano. Three of the tables back there
were occupied, served by a sour waitress in black dress and
white apron.

Two of the women at the bar turned to look at Parker, but
he ignored them and walked farther down where a batch of
stools were empty. He didn't sit down, but stood leaning
against the bar. One of the bartenders came down and asked
him what he'd have.

"Menner of Miami Beach sent me up to see Jim," he said.

"Who?"

"Jim St. Clair."

"No, no, the other one."

"Menner."

The bartender shook his head. He was a burly man gone to fat. He said, "I don't know that name."

Parker shrugged.

The bartender studied him a minute and then said, "I'll see. What'll you have?"

"Budweiser."

"Check." He turned and called to the other barkeep, "Bud, here. I'll be right back."

He walked away, with the busy walk of a bartender—bent forward slightly and working his arms as though he were shoving a beer keg along in front of him. His apron hung almost to his ankles, and it whipped around his feet as he walked. He went down to the end of the bar, raised the flap, went through, and turned right through a door next to the door marked "Pointers." Farther back, there was a door marked "Setters." Both doors had metal dog silhouettes nailed on them.

The other bartender strolled down with the bottle and glass, took Parker's dollar, and brought back a fifty-cent piece. Parker put the coin in his pocket and drank some beer.

The first bartender came back after awhile, leaned on the bar in front of Parker, and said, "Okay. Right through there where I went."

"Good."

Parker walked back, pushed open the door, and found himself in a short bright hallway with plaster cream-colored walls. At the end, where the hall made an *L* to the left, there was a door facing him marked "Office." He walked over to it,

looked to the left, and saw a gleaming kitchen with an un-
dershirted Negro sweating at the clipper. Parker pushed open
the office door and went in.

It was a small, cramped room with gray walls. A desk was
shoved against one wall, a filing cabinet against another, and
there was a water cooler in the corner, leaving a small circle of
black linoleum floor space free in the middle of the room. A
short, fat, red-faced man looked up from the desk on which
there were open ledgers, and asked, "Well? Hah?" He waved
his hands, both covered with ink.

"Menner sent me to see you," Parker told him. He started
to close the door, but the bartender had come along behind
him and was standing there.

The red-faced man was saying, "Menner? Hah? Menner?
Menner's dead."

Parker nodded. "I know. But Cresetti said you didn't know
him, so I should use Menner's name."

"Cresetti? Hah? Who?"

"He took over from Menner."

"And he sent you up here? Why? What the hell do I have
to do with this Cresetti? What's this Cresetti to me?"

"You sent Menner that guy Stern," Parker reminded him.
The bartender was just standing there behind him, leaning
against the doorframe.

"Sure, Stern," said the red-faced man. "Sure, I sent him. He
screwed up, huh? That bastard Parker killed him—how do
you like that?"

Parker shrugged. "He killed Menner, too." He wasn't paying attention, he was trying to decide what to do about the bartender.

"Sure, he killed Menner. They tell me maybe he'll come here." The red-faced man squinted at him. "You think so? Nah, I don't think so. What's he got against me? Menner fingered him, yeah, and Stern tried to knock him off, yeah, but what did I do to the bastard? Nothing. I'm told send a gun to this Menner in Florida. I do it. I don't know what this gun is supposed to do, I don't have nothing to do with nothing. So I figure this bastard won't bother with me. He'll ignore me, right?"

"Maybe," said Parker.

"Maybe you're him," said the red-faced man. "Hah! That's a hot one, huh? Maybe you're him! Maybe I oughta have Johnny frisk you."

"I've got a gun on me."

The man grinned and ducked his head, multiplying his chins. He was full of fun. "Heeled? Hah?"

"Stern's gun," Parker told him. "I'm bringing it back. A .25 with a silencer. Johnny can reach in my right-hand pocket and he'll find it there." Parker waited for Johnny to come up behind him, close enough.

But the red-faced man waved his hands. "Nah, why? We enemies? We animals in a jungle? Just take off the coat, that's all. It's hot in here, who needs a coat? Gimme—I'll hang it up."

Parker shrugged. He took off his coat, handed it toward St. Clair, and dropped it on the floor just before St. Clair got it.

Grunting, St. Clair automatically stooped for it, and Parker kicked him in the face. His hand went inside his suit jacket as he turned, and when it came out it had the stubby .38 in it. Johnny was one step into the room, but he stopped when he saw the gun.

"Back to the door, Johnny," Parker told him. "Lean against the wall like before. Fold your arms. That's a good boy, Johnny."

Johnny stood there the way he was told. His face was expressionless. St. Clair was lying on the floor. Parker tugged on a drawer of the filing cabinet and found it locked. He'd been a little worried when he'd seen no safe in the room, but now he felt better. St. Clair kept his cash in a locked filing cabinet. He felt real sure of himself, St. Clair.

Parker went down on one knee, watching Johnny, and went through St. Clair's pockets till he found a key ring. It would be easier to bring Johnny into the room, put him to sleep, and shut the door, but it might not be smart. The Negro in the kitchen might be primed—he might know that everything was all right only so long as Johnny was standing in the doorway. Parker, when he was working, liked to leave things as they were as much as possible.

Left-handed, he unlocked the filing cabinet, and then started opening and shutting drawers. In the bottom drawer was a green metal box. Parker lifted it out. It was heavy. He put it on the desk and found the key on the ring which opened it. Rolls of coins lined the top tray. He put the tray aside; he had no use for coins. The bottom of the box was full of stacked bills. Parker removed St. Clair's wallet from his jacket pocket and dropped it in the box. He looked at Johnny again. "Yours, too."

Johnny moved very slowly, reaching around under the apron to his hip pocket and coming up with a worn brown leather wallet. Parker said, "Toss it on the desk."

"I got a lot of papers in there," Johnny told him. "Driver's license and stuff."

"Good," said Parker. It would go with the papers from the poker players in Miami. Legitimate papers were always useful. He dropped the wallet in the box and closed the top. Then he switched the gun to his left hand, picked up the box in his right, and swung it against St. Clair's head. It made a dull echoing sound. When St. Clair woke up, he'd be in a hospital.

Parker put the box down, got into his topcoat, and picked the box up again. "Now," he said, "we're going outside. We'll go through the kitchen and out the back way, and you won't say anything to that boy working back there, not even hello. You got me?"

"Not yet, but I will."

"Don't be brave, Johnny, you just work here. Let's go."

Johnny led the way, and Parker followed, cradling the metal box. They went out to the hallway and turned right to go through the kitchen. The Negro was still sweating at the clipper, shoving dirty dishes in at one end and pulling clean dishes out at the other. The clipper made a lot of noise and he didn't even notice them going through. The kitchen was

steamy from the clipper, which made the outside air seem
even colder and damper than before.

After they went out, Parker closed the door. It was pitch-
black, and it took Parker a few seconds for his eyes to adjust.
Then he saw and heard Johnny making a run for it to the left.
He smiled thinly and followed. They both went around the
building, Johnny crashing and blundering ahead, Parker
moving silently in his wake. Then Johnny burst out to the
brightly-lit sidewalk and ducked to the left around the corner
of the building toward the entrance. Parker made it to the
sidewalk and walked the other way. In three steps he was in
darkness, and then he was around the corner. He got into the
Olds, put the metal box on the seat beside him, and drove
away.

4

In spidery Gothic script, the name plate on the ivory door read:

Justin
Fairfax

Parker looked at the name, then touched his finger to the button beside the door. The apartment within was sound-proofed. Standing in the muted hall, Parker couldn't hear the bell or chimes or whatever sound the button produced. Probably chimes. He waited, looking at the name plate on the door.

Justin Fairfax. He hadn't moved. That was stupid, it really was. He should have moved.

Parker had been here once before, while trying to get his money back from the syndicate. Justin Fairfax was one of the two men in charge of the New York area of the Outfit's operations.

The door opened. A heavy-set, distrustful man stood there, his right hand near his jacket lapel. He asked quietly, "What is it?"

Beyond him, Parker could see the elegant living room with its white broadloom carpet, white leather sofa, and free-form glass coffee table. The twin brothers of the heavy-set man lounged there, looking out of place, like burglars resting in the middle of a heist.

"I've got the message for Mr. Fairfax. From Jim St. Clair," Parker said.

"What's the message?"

"I'm supposed to deliver it to him personally."

"Tough. What's the message?"

Parker shrugged. "I'll go tell Mr. St. Clair you wouldn't let me in," he said. He turned away and headed for the elevator.

"Hold on."

Parker looked back.

"All right. You wait there, I'll see what Mr. Fairfax has to say."

"I'll wait inside. I don't want to hang around the hallway."

The heavy-set man made an angry face. "All right," he said, "get in here."

Parker went in, and the heavy-set man closed the door after him. They stepped down into the living room, and the man warned, "Watch this bird!" Then he crossed the room and went through another door which led deeper into the apartment.

The twin brothers watched him. Parker stood with his hand in his pockets, his right hand on the .38. His topcoat was unbuttoned, so he could aim the gun in any direction from within the pocket.

The heavy-set man came back, followed by Fairfax. Fairfax was tall and stately, graying at the temples, with a smartly clipped pepper-and-salt moustache. He was about fifty-five, and had obviously spent a lot of time in gymnasiums. He was wearing a silk Japanese robe and wicker sandals. He looked at Parker and frowned. "Do I know you?"

The new face came in handy sometimes. Parker said, "I work for Mr. St. Clair. You might of seen me around with him."

"Mmmmm." Fairfax touched his moustache with the tips of his fingers. "Well, what's the message?"

Parker glanced meaningfully at the bodyguards. "Mr. St. Clair said I should keep it private."

"You can speak in front of these men."

"Well—it has to do with Parker."

Fairfax smiled thinly. "Parker is the reason these men are here," he said. "What about him?"

"He knocked over The Three Kings tonight."

"He what?"

"He beat up Mr. St. Clair and the bartender. He walked off with thirty-four hundred dollars."

"So he's in New York." Fairfax mused, stroking his moustache.

"He told Mr. St. Clair he was coming to see you next."

"He did, eh?" Fairfax glanced around at his three bodyguards. He smiled again, with scornful amusement. "I think
we're ready for him if he does come," he said. "Don't you?"

"No."

Parker fired through his pocket, and the heavy-set man
who had let him in staggered back one step and fell over a
table, scattering magazines to the floor. The twin brothers
jumped to their feet, but Parker pulled the gun from his
pocket and they stopped, frozen in midgesture. Fairfax
backed up until his shoulders brushed the far wall; his face
was pale and haggard, and his fingers now covered his moustache completely.

Parker ordered the twins, "Pick him up. Fairfax, lead the
way. Same bedroom as last time." The last time he had been
here, there'd been bodyguards, too. They'd been locked in a
bedroom while Parker said what he had to say.

The twins went over to the man on the floor. One of them
looked up, saying, "He isn't dead."

"I know. I caught him in the shoulder. You can call a doc-
tor after I leave here."

Fairfax, looking stunned, led the way. The brothers followed, carrying the wounded man, and Parker came last.
They went into the bedroom and the twins put the wounded
man down on the bed. Fairfax pursed his lips at that, but
didn't say anything.

Parker said, "Guns on the floor. Move very slow and easy, and one at a time. You first."

They did as they were told. Then Parker had them stand a few feet back from the wall, leaning on their hands, bodies off balance. He frisked them, finding nothing more on them. He relieved the wounded man of his gun, picked up the three guns in his left hand by their trigger guards, and motioned Fairfax to precede him out of the bedroom. Parker locked the door behind him. He and Fairfax went back to the living room.

Fairfax had regained some of his composure. "I don't know what you hope to gain," he said. "You'll keep annoying us, and we'll keep hunting you. The end is inevitable."

"Wrong. You aren't hunting me, I'm hunting you. Right now, I'm hunting Bronson."

"You won't get at him as readily as you got at me."

"Let me worry about that. This is the second time I've met up with you, Fairfax, and you can live through it this time too, if you cooperate."

"Whatever you want, it's beyond my power to give it to you."

"No, it isn't. I want two things. I want to know where Bronson is now and where he'll be for the next week or two. And I want to know who in the Outfit is slated to take over if anything happens to Bronson."

Fairfax's smile was shaky. "It would be worth my life to tell you either of those things."

"You won't have any life left if you don't. I got your bodyguards out of the way so you could tell me without anybody knowing. I'm making it easy on you."

"I'm sorry. This time you'll just have to kill me." His voice had a quaver in it, but he met Parker's eyes and he kept his hand away from his moustache.

Parker considered. Then he said, "All right, we'll make it easier than that. You know who's next in line after Bronson. I want to get in touch with him."

"Why?"

"You listen, and you'll find out. What's his name?"

Fairfax thought it over. His hand came up stealthily and lingered at his moustache. He said, finally, as though to himself, "You want to make a deal. All right, there's no harm in that. It's Walter Karns."

"Can you call him now?"

"I imagine he's at his place in Los Angeles."

"Phone him."

Fairfax got on the phone. Karns wasn't at the first two places he tried. Fairfax finally got in touch with him in Seattle, and said, "Hold on a second." He hadn't identified himself.

Parker took the phone. "Karns?"

"Yes?" It was a rich voice, a brandy-and-cigar voice. "Who is it?"

"I'm Parker. Ever hear of me?"

"Parker? The Parker who's been causing all that trouble in the East?"

"That's the one."

"Well, well, well. To what do I owe the honor?"

"If anything happens to Bronson, you're in, right?"

"What? Well, now, you're going a little fast there, aren't you?"

"I'm going after Bronson. Maybe I can make a deal with him, so we'll both be satisfied."

"I really doubt that, you know."

"Maybe I can, maybe I can't. If I don't, you're next in line. What I want to know is should I spend any time talking to Bronson?"

"Well, well! So that's it!"

"Do I try to make a deal with Bronson?"

"He'll never do it, you know."

"You got any other reasons why I shouldn't try?"

"Hold on. Let me think about this."

Parker held on. After a minute, Karns said, "I think we could probably work something out, Parker."

"You people go your way, I go mine. You don't annoy me, I don't annoy you."

"That certainly sounds reasonable."

"Yeah. Give me a guarantee."

"A guarantee? Well, now. Yes, I see your position, of course, but—a guarantee. I'm not sure I know what guarantee I could give you."

"Right now, the Outfit is out to get me. If you take over, what happens?"

"After this conversation? If I take over, as you say, as a result of any activity on your part, I assure you I'll be grateful.

The organization would no longer bother you in any way. As to what *guarantee* I could give you—"

"Never mind. I'll give you a guarantee. I'll get Bronson. I got Carter—you remember him?"

"From New York? Yes, I remember that clearly."

"And I had my hands on Fairfax once. And, now, I'll get Bronson. That means, if I have to, I can find you, too."

"You seem to have found me already. Who was that on the phone before you?"

"That's not part of the deal. I just want you to understand the situation."

"I think I understand, Parker. Believe me, if you succeed in ending the career of Arthur Bronson, you will have my undying respect and admiration. I would no more cross you thereafter than I would shake hands with a scorpion."

Parker motioned for Fairfax to come close. Into the phone, he said, "Say it plain and simple. If I get Bronson, what?"

He held the phone out toward Fairfax. They both heard the faint voice say, "If you get Arthur Bronson, Mr. Parker, the organization will never bother you again."

Parker brought the phone back to his mouth and said, "That's good. Good-by, Mr. Karns."

"Good-by, Mr. Parker. And, good hunting!"

Parker hung up. He turned to Fairfax. "Well?"

Fairfax stroked his moustache. "I've always admired Karns," he said. "And I never did like Bronson. You'll find him in Buffalo. He's staying at his wife's house until you're found. 798 Delaware, facing the park."

"All right, Fairfax. Now listen. What happens if you warn Bronson?"

"I won't, you can rely on that."

"But what happens if you do? You have to let him know you told me where to find him. He wouldn't take any excuse at all for that."

"I'm not going to warn him."

"What about those bodyguards of yours? Can you keep them quiet about tonight?"

"They work for me, not for Bronson."

"All right." Parker went to the hall door and opened it. "Good-by, Fairfax."

"Good-by."

Parker boarded the elevator and rode down. He walked out onto Fifth Avenue. Central Park was in front of him and the Olds was illegally parked around the corner. He plucked the green ticket from under the windshield wiper, ripped it in two, and dropped the pieces in the gutter. Then he got behind the wheel. First to Scranton to pick up Handy McKay, if Handy felt like coming, and then on to Buffalo.

THREE

Three

1

Rolling slow and silent beside the park in the late-morning sunlight, the two black Cadillacs formed a convoy that moved at measured pace along the black-top street. Dappled sunlight filtered through the parkside trees reflecting semaphoric highlights from the polished chrome. Alone in the rear seat of the second Cadillac, Arthur Bronson chewed sourly on his cigar and glowered out in distaste at the beautiful day. The late November air was crisp, clean, and cold, the late November sunlight bright and shimmering. A few scarlet leaves still clung to some of the trees along the park's edge relieving the stark blackness of their trunks and branches.

A hell of a place to be in November! he thought, thinking of Las Vegas. He glanced ahead, saw his wife's house and repeated the thought: *A hell of a place to be in November. A hell of a place to be anytime.*

It was a big stone monstrosity of a house facing the park.

Twenty-one rooms, tall narrow windows, three stories, four staircases, impossible to heat. Putting in decent wiring and plumbing had cost a fortune. Buying statues to fill the niches and paintings for the walls had cost another fortune. And then rugs. And half the furniture on the Eastern Seaboard. For what? For a house he inhabited not more than three months out of the year unless something unusual came up.

But Willa had wanted it. She was a Buffalo girl, from the cracked-sidewalk section back of Civic Center, and owning one of these stone piles by the park had been her driving ambition for as long as she could remember. And what Willa wanted, whatever she truly wanted, Arthur Bronson went out and got for her.

He was fifty-six, born in Baltimore seven years before World War I and thirteen years before Prohibition. He'd been driving a rum-runner's truck at fourteen, in charge of collection in the northeast area of Washington at twenty, one of the four most powerful men in the Baltimore-Washington area liquor syndicate at twenty-seven when Prohibition ended. He was the most powerful man in that area at thirty-two, member of the national committee from the mid-East states at thirty-nine. He had become chairman of the committee at forty-seven and had held that post for the past nine years.

His cover was impeccable. He was senior partner in a Buffalo firm of investment counselors, with a junior partner who handled all the legitimate business. He was a member of Kenmore, a suburb. He belonged to a country club and a businessmen's fraternal organization; he was a member in good standing of the church three blocks from his Buffalo home, and his income tax returns would never send him to jail. At fifty-six, he was of medium height, about twenty pounds overweight, and his black hair was flecked distinguishedly with gray. His face was broad and somewhat puffy, but he still retained traces of his earlier dark good looks. He gave the impression of being a solid citizen, a hard businessman, possibly a difficult employer, but absolutely respectable.

Willa, too, was respectable. In 1930, when he'd married her, she'd been a mediocre singer with a fair jazz band, but she took to rich respectability as though she'd known no other life. She was now fifty-two, a plump and soft-spoken matron, a doting grandmother who was constantly phoning her married daughter in San Jose, to find out how her two grandsons were getting on. The pile of stones facing the park was her home twelve months out of the year. Her husband might be away for months at a time—New York, Las Vegas, Mexico City, Naples—but this pile of stones was Willa's home, and she stayed in it.

It was not her husband's home, and he avoided it as much as possible. He didn't like the place, it was too big, too solemn, too empty, too drafty, too far removed from life. He preferred hotel suites with terraces overlooking a pool or the sea. He preferred chrome and red leather. When it came to that, he preferred a good, stacked, intelligent, hundred-dollar whore on a white leather sofa to the plump grandmother in the pile of stones in Buffalo, but, at the same time, it was the good whore who got the hundred dollars and the plump grandmother who got the hundred-thousand-dollar house.

The lead Cadillac crawled on past the driveway and stopped. There were four men in the car, and they looked out the windows intently in all directions, watching the traffic and pedestrians. The second Cadillac with the armed colored chauffeur at the wheel and Bronson alone in the back seat turned in the driveway like a sleek tank. Only after it had gone in past the hedge did the other Cadillac go on down the street and around the corner. To the undiscerning eye, there was no particular connection between the two Cadillacs.

The black-top drive looped past the front of the house, then curved round to the garage at the side. The chauffeur stopped at the front door and hopped out to open the door for Bronson. Bronson climbed out and the chauffeur asked, "You want the car any more today?"

"No." It was said angrily. Where the hell was there to go? He'd just come from the funeral of a local businessman, the owner of a chain of supermarkets. Funerals. Big, dark, stone houses. Cold weather. All because of one madman named Parker. He went up the steps and into the house, and the chauffeur took the Cadillac around to the garage. Another driveway came in from behind the garage, and the second Cadillac came in that way. The two of them were put away and the five men went into the house through one of the back doors.

Bronson, passing through the main hall, found his wife in the small room behind the drawing room watching television.

He stood in the doorway, feeling grumpy, but not wanting to take it out on Willa. It wasn't *her* fault. He said, "Hello."

"Oh, hello!" She got to her feet, a plump, pleasant-looking woman with timid mannerisms, and went over to turn the television off.

"Let it go," he said. "What's on?"

"It's just a movie. I think there might be a football game on one of the other channels." She wasn't used to having her husband home. She was grateful for his presence, but at the same time she knew he wasn't here of his own free will. What the problem that had forced him home was she didn't know—he never talked about his business with her—but she knew it had to be something serious. Every once in a while during the year he would stop in for a few days, just long enough to put in token appearances at his office downtown and at a few business luncheons or civic meetings, then he would be off again. But this time was different. This time, he was obviously angry and upset, as though it hadn't been his original plan to come at this time. And he had brought all those bodyguards with him, a thing he'd never done before. So she knew he was here against his will and she worried about it, wondering what she could do to make his stay less difficult. "I'll see if I can find that football game."

"No, never mind. You watch your movie."

"Are you sure?"

"I'm sure. I'm sure."

She wilted at the tone, immediately looking sheepish. "I'm sorry, Arthur."

"Oh, for Christ's sake! I'm not mad at you."

"I know, Arthur. I—"

One of the bodyguards appeared in the doorway. "Phone, Mr. Bronson."

"All right." He was grateful for the interruption. He left the room and hurried upstairs.

Could this be it? Had they run Parker down? Could he now get the hell away from this mausoleum?

At the head of the stairs on the second floor, a hall as wide as many of the rooms stretched away to his left, lawned with Persian and lined with candelabras. He walked down this hall, the carpet muffling his tread, and entered the third room on the right—his office.

The office was dominated by a desk the size of a sports car, carefully wrought of hand-carved Honduras mahogany. Books he had bought—not to read, but because they were in sets with bindings of which the decorator had approved—lined the shelves on three walls. Two tall narrow windows faced the tree-lined street and the park beyond.

Bronson sat at the desk and reached out for the telephone, hoping it was the good news he'd been waiting for. He checked the movement at the last second, wanting to prolong the suspense, and made the caller wait while he unwrapped and lit a cigar. The cigar in his left hand, he reached out for the phone again.

But it wasn't good news. It was bad news, very bad news. Someone had just knocked off the Club Cockatoo.

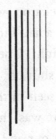

2

The neon sign which hung out by the road was green. It said:

CLUB

C
O
C
K
A
T
O
O

DANCING

Town was five miles away to the east, along the two-lane
black-top road, moving gradually down the decline into the

valley where the city was situated. From that direction came an orange Volkswagen. The driver was alone in the car, a bulky canvas-covered bundle lay on the back seat. It putted by the Club Cockatoo, with the characteristic cough of the VW. A mile and a half further along there was an Esso station, closed for the night. The VW putted in there and stopped. The lights were shut off. The low, small silhouette of the car could hardly be seen in the dark—couldn't be seen at all unless you knew it was there. The driver, a short thin man named Rico, got out and walked back down the road toward the Club Cockatoo.

It was a Saturday night, so the parking lot was crowded. Rico walked through the ranks of cars to the line parked facing the side of the building. There was a door on the side, near the rear, and Rico headed for that. The car nearest that side door was a white Ford Thunderbird. Rico tried the door on the driver's side, found it locked, and shrugged in irritation. Then he tried the next car, a dark green Continental. The door was unlocked. He stood next to it, waiting.

After a minute, a black Buick, two years old and stolen that afternoon, turned into the parking lot. The driver was alone in the Buick. He was tall and slender, about forty, with a pock-marked face. His name was Terry. He nodded when he saw Rico.

Rico looked at the Buick, then got behind the wheel of the Continental. He bent and fiddled under the dashboard for a minute. Then the engine started, and he backed the Continental out of its place. He headed it around several lanes toward another parking space. The Buick nosed forward and slid into the vacant spot. Rico fiddled under the dashboard on the Continental again, and the engine stopped. He got out and walked over to the Buick. Terry got out and they both walked around to the front and entered the club. They wore dark suits and ties, and took their hats off as they stepped through the entrance.

This was an Outfit operation, a rambling cream stucco structure two stories high. It was in a dry county where liquor is illegal, in one of the forty-nine states in which gambling is illegal, and in one of the fifty in which prostitution and narcotics are illegal.

The only legal activity going on in the Club Cockatoo was dancing. On the first floor was the bar, where every drink ever heard of in New York City was available—at a price a little higher than in New York City. The waiters and bartenders had decks of marijuana for sale; the stronger drugs had never really caught on in that part of the country. Upstairs were the beds, and the maidens who manned them. And downstairs were the games. It was a good operation, profitable and safe. The local law was well-greased, and there had been no problems. Not until tonight.

No building is safe from robbery, if a professional can get his hands on the blueprints. There were a few basic flaws in this particular building—from a robbery-proof viewpoint—that the Outfit had never considered before, but would have an opportunity to consider tonight.

The side door. It led to a short hallway, which, in turn, led to the bar. This hallway also opened onto a flight of stairs which led down to the gambling room. A man going down these stairs would find himself in another hallway with a barred window on his left and the main gambling room to his right. Directly across the hall, he would see the doors to the rest rooms. Turning to the right and entering the main room, he would see that it was filled with tables of various kinds, and that along one wall there was a wire wicket, like a teller's cage in a bank, except that the wire enclosure extended to the ceiling. Behind this were the cashiers, with drawers full of money and chips. And behind the cashiers was a wall with a door in it. Turning around and going back to the hallway and thence to the men's room, he would discover that the men's room and the cashiers' space shared a wall, and that the door he had already noticed led into the men's room. This door was kept locked; it could be unlocked from either side only by a key. Each cashier had a key which he was required to turn in when going off duty. The arrangement had been designed as a convenience to the cashiers, who worked long hours and were permitted an occasional beer.

And the office. It was behind the cashiers' wicket, to the left of the men's room. The door to the office was about eight feet to the left of the private door to the men's room. This door was not kept locked; because the cashiers used it fairly often, clearing checks, bringing money in or taking money out, coming on or going off duty. The office was windowless, having an air-conditioner high on the outside wall, and the door to the cashiers' space was its only entrance. The three men who worked in the office were armed.

Rico and Terry entered the club and stopped at the bar long enough for a bottle of beer, then they went downstairs to the gambling room. They entered the men's room. Each went quickly into a stall and closed the door, and then they both put on rubber masks which covered their faces completely. The masks had two oval eyeholes and two round nostril holes, and for the rest were flesh-colored rubber, loosely fitted to the contours of their faces. They put their hats on over the masks and waited. Patrons came and went.

They waited forty minutes before they heard the sound of a cashier's key. They heard a door open and close, they heard footsteps on the floor. They came out of the stalls.

They each had guns now—stubby English .32's. The cashier was a small, bald man with spectacles which reflected the light. He wore a white shirt with the sleeves rolled up, and his forearms were thin and pale and almost hairless.

There was one other customer in the room, washing his hands at one of the sinks. Terry, the pock-marked man, pointed a gun at him. "Come over here."

Rico went over to the cashier. "Turn around. Put your palms against the wall." Then he patted pockets till he found the key.

They marched the cashier and the customer into adjoining stalls and made them kneel down. The cashier was silent, but the customer kept babbling they could have his wallet without killing him. Rico and Terry sapped them and lowered them gently to the tile floor. If there were no killings and no injuries needing hospital care, there would probably be no official squawk from this job. The club wouldn't be making any reports to the law if it could avoid it. And the customer would probably be paid off if he raised a stink on his own. If the job was clean and quiet, the law would never hear about it at all.

They closed the stall doors and went to the private door. Rico unlocked it and led the way through. They had the guns in their pockets now, their right hands tucked into the same pockets.

To the right was a long table. Felt-lined boxes full of chips were stacked up on the table, and empty ones were under the table. To the left was another table which held adding machines, telephones, and a few single-drawer filing cabinets for three-by-five cards. Beyond that table was the door to the office. In front stretched the counter and the wire cage. All but one of the cashiers had their backs to them. This one sat at the table to the left, running an adding machine. He looked over when Rico and Terry came through the doorway, and his eyes widened. He was the only one who could see the masks; the other cashiers were facing away and the customers and stickmen beyond the wire mesh were too far away to see what was happening. Anyone looking through the wicket toward the dim area by the back wall wouldn't realize that those pale expressionless faces weren't faces at all.

Speaking softly, Rico said to the man at the adding machine, "Come here. Be nice and quiet." There was a steady flow of noise from beyond the wire, the rustle of conversation and the clatter of chips. None of the other cashiers heard Rico's voice.

The man at the adding machine slowly got to his feet. He understood now, and he was terrified. He was blinking rapidly behind his glasses, and his hands gripped each other at his waist. He came over slowly.

Rico said, "Stand in front of me." Rico pulled out the gun and showed it to him. "My partner has one, too."

The man nodded convulsively.

"What's your name?" That was part of his pattern, Rico always wanted to know the name. He said it was psychological, it calmed the victim down and made him less likely to do something stupid out of panic, but that was just an excuse, something Rico had thought up. He wanted to know the name, that was all.

"Stewart. Rob—Robert Stewart."

"All right, Bob. We're cleaning this place. We want to do it quiet, we don't want your customers all shook up. And we don't want the cops coming down here and seeing all the wheels and everything. You don't want that either, right?"

Stewart nodded again. He was staring at Rico's mouth, watching his lips move behind the rubber mask, making it tremble.

"Now, Bob, the three of us are going to walk into the office. Smile, Bob. I want to see you smile."

Stewart stretched his lips. From a distance, it might look like a smile.

"That's the way. Now keep smiling while we go into the office." Rico tucked the gun away into his pocket again, but kept his hand on it. "Here we go, Bob."

Stewart turned around and led the way to the left, Rico following him, and Terry bringing up the rear. They walked into the office, Stewart smiling his strained smile, and Terry closed the door and leaned against it. Rico pulled his gun out again, shoved Stewart to the side, and said, "I'm looking for heroes."

A man was squatting in front of the safe, his hands full of stacked bills. A second man was at the desk, a pencil in his right hand, his left holding a telephone to his ear. A third man was at a table entering figures in a ledger. They all looked up and froze.

Rico pointed the gun at the man holding the phone. "Something just came up. I'll call you back."

The man with the telephone repeated the words and hung up. The man at the safe kept licking his lips and glancing at the safe door. He was trying to build up the courage to slam the door. Rico pointed the gun at him. "You—what's your name?"

"What?" He'd been concentrating on the gun and the safe door, and he couldn't understand the question.

"Your name. What's your name?"

He looked over at the man at the desk, appealing to him. The man at the desk said, "Tell him."

"J—Jim."

"All right, Jim. Stand up straight. That's good. Take two steps to your left. Very nice, Jim." Rico took two canvas sacks from under his coat and handed them to Stewart. "What you do, Bob," he said, "you go over and empty that safe. Put all the loot in these sacks. Jim, you give Bob that money you're holding. You—" he pointed the gun again at the man at the desk. "What's your name?"

"Fred Kirk." He was a heavy, florid man, probably the manager, since he was the only one who didn't seem to be frightened.

"All right, Fred. If that phone rings, say you can't talk now. You've got a problem here. You'll call back."

"You won't get three miles."

"Quiet now, Fred."

"Don't you know who runs this place? You guys are crazy."

"No more talk, Fred. Don't make me put you to sleep. You—" He turned to the man at the ledger. "What's your name, partner?"

"Kelway. Stanley Kelway." His quavering voice was high and thin.

"Now, don't get upset, Stan. You just keep making them entries."

"I can't." Kelway was perspiring heavily. He kept moving his hands, shifting the pen back and forth from one to the other.

"Too nervous, Stan? All right, just sit there easy."

Stewart came back with the two canvas sacks, both bulging now, nearly too heavy for him to carry. He held them out to Rico, but Rico shook his head. "Oh, no, Bob, you'll carry them. Fred, you'll wait till Bob gets back before you make a fuss or Bob won't be coming back. You wouldn't want a corpse on the property, would you, Fred?"

Kirk glowered.

"All right, Bob, let's go."

Terry went first, opening the door and stepping out quickly, looking both ways. The cashiers still worked along, unconcerned, their backs to the action. Beyond the mesh, the customers and the stickmen concentrated on their own business. Terry moved to the right. Stewart followed him, carrying the sacks. Rico backed out, closed the door and pocketed the gun.

There were two customers in the men's room and when they saw the masked men they raised their hands without being asked. Rico closed the door and said, "Bob here is an employee. Aren't you, Bob?"

Stewart nodded.

"Bob will come back in a minute and explain the whole thing. In the meantime, he'd like you to stay right here and not raise any sort of fuss. For your own good, that is. And for his. Isn't that right, Bob?"

Stewart nodded again.

"You don't have to keep your hands up like that, boys. Just stay here and wait. It'll only be a couple minutes. But if you try to leave here too soon, you might just possibly get shot. Isn't that right, Bob?"

Stewart licked his lips. "Do like they say," he said. "They got guns. Just do like they say."

"Don't worry," said one of the customers.

Terry, Rico, and Stewart left the men's room, crossed the hall, and went up the stairs. Terry opened the side door and checked outside, then nodded to Rico. He never talked during a job, unless it was absolutely necessary. Rico did all the talking for both of them.

Rico took the two sacks from Stewart. "All right, Bob," he said. "You did that real well. You can go back downstairs now."

Stewart hurried back downstairs. His shoulders were hunched, like he believed he would be shot anyway.

Rico and Terry went over and got into the Buick. Rico got behind the wheel and Terry sat beside him. The canvas sacks were on the floor between Terry's legs. Rico backed the Buick out of the slot and headed for the highway. They both still had the masks on.

Terry turned, looking back at the club. Just as Rico reached the road, Terry saw the side door open and four men come running out. Two of them pointed frantically at the Buick. Terry said, "They spotted us."

"Good for them," said Rico. He spun the wheel and the Buick cut left, then leaped down the highway. Behind them, the four men were piling into a Chrysler Imperial. Rico accelerated and the Buick streaked along. He switched off the headlights as soon as he saw the station ahead. "Here they come, Rico."

"Sure."

Rico cut the wheel and switched off the ignition, and the Buick slid silently up beside the orange Volkswagen.

They were out of the Buick before it had completely stopped. They grabbed the sacks and jumped out. The sacks they tossed behind the front seat of the Volkswagen. Hats and masks followed. Then they both got into the car, slamming the doors.

The Chrysler Imperial shot by, and went about a hundred yards further down the road before its brakes began to squeal. Rico started the VW, spun it around in a tight turn, and aimed it toward town. It didn't shift like a Volkswagen, and, above sixty miles an hour, it didn't sound much like a Volkswagen any more. Two more cars came boiling out of the Club Cockatoo and roared by the little orange car without a glance. Everybody knows a VW is no good as a getaway car.

This wasn't the operation Rico had ordered the VW for, but just before he'd picked up the car he'd received the letter from Parker about hitting the syndicate. The Club Cockatoo had been bothering him for seven years, and he felt relieved when he discovered a justifiable reason for knocking it over. He combined the plan he already had with the orange car he'd just picked up, brought Terry into the deal, and did the job immediately, before Parker could tell him everything had been straightened out. He drove along now pleased with Parker, pleased with the car, pleased with the operation, pleased with the world.

By morning, they were nearly six hundred miles away from the club, so they stopped to see just how much they'd taken.

3

"**E**ighty-seven Grand!"

Bronson stared at the telephone. He didn't believe it. It was a bad dream.

The voice at the other end was saying, "Just two guys, Mr. Bronson. They came in and did the job like they'd been practicing it for ten years."

"Where the hell was everybody? Asleep?"

"Mr. Bronson, these guys were smooth. They came in and—"

"God damn it, Kirk, don't give me a lot of crap! How many employees you got?"

"Thirty-seven, Mr. Bronson."

"Where the hell were they?"

"All working, Mr. Bronson. Most of them didn't even know what was going on. They sapped a cashier and a customer, and held—"

"They sapped a customer? How much did that cost me, Kirk?"

"Half a yard. He—"

"Another five hundred. Pretty goddamn expensive, Kirk."

"We didn't want any stink, Mr. Bronson. We—"

"How many people know about this, Kirk?"

"Just me and maybe seven employees and three customers. I called—"

"*Three* customers?"

"Two more saw them on the way out. But I straightened that out, Mr. Bronson. And then I called Marty Keller, and he said I should call you direct."

"He gave you the number, huh?"

"Yes, sir, Mr. Bronson. He said you'd want to hear about it right away."

"All right. All right. I'll be sending somebody down there—hold on a second."

"Yes, sir, Mr. Bronson."

Bronson thought a minute, rubbing his hand over his face. "Quill. Jack Quill. He'll be down there in a couple days."

"Yes, sir, Mr. Bronson. I'm sorry about this, Mr. Bronson, but they pulled it off so smooth and quick, and we never ran into nothing like this before."

"All right, Kirk."

"I could maybe of tried to make a play for them before they got out of the club, but I figured then there'd be shooting, maybe a customer killed or something, and that would of been even worse. I figured we'd pick them up after they got outside, but they just disappeared on us. We found the car they used, but they—"

"All right, Kirk. You tell Quill all about it."

"Yes, sir. I'm sorry, Mr. Bron—"

"Good-by, Kirk."

Bronson hung up, then picked his cigar from the ashtray and puffed on it a while, staring at the opposite wall. So it wasn't crap after all. Parker could do it. Somehow or other, he could talk a bunch of heavy armor people into going after organization targets. God *damn* him! How the hell could they guard against a thing like that?

After a while he sighed, put the cigar down again, and picked up the telephone. He dialed an area code, then a seven-digit number. He gave his own number to the operator and listened to the ring that followed.

Keller himself answered. Bronson said, "This is Art."

"Art! Say, did Kirk—"

"You gave out my number, Marty."

"What? Oh! Listen, I just thought you'd want to—"

"You give out my number again, Marty. I retire you. With flowers, Marty."

"Well, sure, Art. Jesus, I figured this was a special—"

"With flowers, Marty."

Bronson slammed the phone down. He glared at it a few seconds, then picked it up, and dialed another number. When he got an answer, he asked to speak to Quill. When Quill came on, he said, "Get on a plane. Come to Buffalo. Phone Edgewood 5-6598 when you get in. Ask for Fred."

"Right now, Mr. Bronson?"

"When the hell do you think, Quill? Next year?"

He broke the connection. The next time he dialed a local number. The voice that came on said, "Circle Rental."

"Let me talk to Fred."

"Who wants him?"

"I do. Snap it up."

There was a silence, then the phone was slammed down. After a brief wait, a new voice came on. "Yeah?"

"Bronson. Sometime tonight or tomorrow, a guy named Quill will call you from the airport. Go pick him up and bring him here."

"Will do."

"Good."

Bronson hung up and spent a while sitting motionless at the desk. He finished his cigar, sat a while longer, then made one more phone call, this time to Fairfax in New York. When Fairfax came on the line, Bronson said, "Parker's causing some more trouble."

"St. Clair's conscious," Fairfax said. "They say he'll pull through."

"What? Who cares? Two professionals knocked over a gambling setup of ours tonight."

"You mean Parker's threat of—"

"I mean two pros knocked over one of our operations! You got wax in your ears?"

"All right, Art, all right. Just take it easy."

"The hell with take it easy! What have we got, god damn

it, do we have an organization or don't we? Do we have twelve thousand employees, coast to coast, or don't we? What the hell is this? One lousy man can goose us any time he wants?"

"You sure this was connected with Parker, Art?"

"Who else?"

"Parker was just in New York two days ago."

"For Christ's sake, do you listen or do you just stand there and play with your moustache? This wasn't Parker, this was two of Parker's friends! You know what that means?"

"Art, did they *say* so? Now, quit screaming at me for a minute. Did they *say* it had anything to do with Parker? Maybe it was somebody else altogether—"

"No. Amateurs try to hit us sometimes, but not pros. Pros leave us alone. Why should two pros suddenly hit us? You like coincidence, maybe?"

"All right, so it was Parker himself, faking it. Right now he's on a plane to Oregon, maybe, or Maine, or someplace, and tomorrow night he does it again. And you stick pins in a map and say, 'Look at that, all over the country. It couldn't all be just one man.' "

"Maybe so."

"Sure. Those robbery guys are loners. They don't go help somebody for the hell of it."

"Yeah. And what the hell difference does it make?"

"What?"

"If Parker's doing it, or somebody else is doing it, what the hell difference does it make? *Somebody's* doing it! We still got hit for eighty-seven grand last night!"

"Well, all I was saying was—"

"Don't give me a lot of talk! I didn't call you so you should give me a lot of theories—who needs them?"

"All right, Art, it's your dime."

"It's a hell of a lot more than a dime, you bastard. Don't get snotty with me."

"I'm not Parker, Art. Shout at him if you want, don't shout at me."

"All right. Wait. Wait a minute." Bronson put the phone down and took a deep breath. He rubbed his hand over his face. He lifted the instrument again and said, "All right, I just got upset, that's all."

"Sure, Art. What did you want?"

"Parker. I want Parker. Don't that sound easy? He's one miserable man, and I'm a coast-to-coast organization. Don't it sound easy?"

"But it isn't easy."

"I know that. All right. What about this Parker? What about his background? Where's he from? Where's he live? What kind of family? He's got to have some family some-place."

"He had a wife, but she's dead. He killed her himself."

"There's got to be somebody. I need a hook in him. I need to be able to grab him. Listen, you put people on it. I want to know who this guy Parker is. I want to know where he's soft."

"I don't think he's soft anywhere."

"Everybody is. Everybody's soft somewhere. We're an organization, right? Can't we find one man? Find me this bastard Parker. Find what he is, what he does, who he knows."

"I'll do my best, Art."

"Don't do your best, god damn you! *Find* him!"

"All right, Art, calm down. I'll call you back tomorrow or the next day."

"Just find him."

He hung up and sat a while longer at the desk, brooding. Then he got to his feet and left the office. He was remembering how abrupt he'd been with Willa, and he wanted to make it up to her. She was somewhere in one of these drafty rooms, maybe still down at the television set. He'd find her and they could go for a drive. Maybe up to the Falls. And stop someplace for dinner. And leave the damn bodyguards behind for once.

He stopped, halfway down the stairs, and thought it over. There was no sense going overboard. Just keep the bodyguards in the other Cad, like this morning. It would be almost the same. Willa would hardly even know they were there.

4

Three days after the Cockatoo Club raid, and twelve hundred miles away—

All the money came to the Novelty Amusement Corporation. It started as small change, here and there throughout the city, and it all funneled into one central office, all the money bet every day on the numbers.

Take one dime. A lady goes into a magazine store and tells the man at the counter she wants to put ten cents on 734. If 734 hits she wins sixty dollars. The odds are 999 to one, but the pay-off is 600 to one. The magazine store owner writes 734 and 10¢ under it on two slips of paper. He gives the woman one slip; he puts the other in a cigar box under the counter. He puts the dime into the cash register, but he rings *No Sale*. At three o'clock, his wife takes over at the counter while he takes the cigar box in back and adds up the amounts on all the slips. The amount is $18.60. He puts all the slips

in an envelope and goes out to the cash register and from it
he takes a ten dollar bill, a five, three ones, two quarters, and
the dime. He puts this cash in the envelope with the slips. He
places the envelope inside a science fiction magazine—on
Wednesdays, it's a science fiction magazine—and puts the
magazine under the counter.

At three-thirty, the collector comes. The collector is a
plump young man with a smiling face, a struggling writer
making a few dollars while waiting to be discovered by Dar-
ryl Zanuck or Bennett Cerf. He drives up in a seven-year-old
Plymouth that belongs to the local numbers organization and
which he is allowed to drive only while making collections.
He parks in front of the magazine store, goes inside, and asks
for a copy of a particular science fiction magazine. The owner
gives him the magazine and tells him that will be $1.86. No
science fiction magazine in the world costs $1.86, but that's
what the young man hands over with no protest.

The young man then carries the magazine out to the car.
He sits behind the wheel, takes the envelope from the magazine, puts it in a briefcase which is on the seat beside him. He
tosses the magazine onto the back seat with seven other dis-
carded magazines and taking a small notebook from his breast
pocket, he writes in it after several other entries: "MPL 1.86."
Then he puts the notebook and pencil away and drives on to
his next stop.

All in all, he buys fifteen magazines, then drives on to the
Kenilworth Building and leaves the car in the lot next door.
He carries the briefcase up to the seventh floor and enters the

offices of the Novelty Amusement Corporation. He smiles at the receptionist, who never gives him a tumble, and goes into the second door on the right, where a sallow man with a cigarette dangling from his lips nods bleakly. The young man puts briefcase and notebook on the desk, and sits down to wait.

The sallow man has an adding machine on his desk. He opens the notebook and adds the figures for the day, coming up with $32.31, which should be ten percent of the day's take. He then adds up the prices on the policy slips, and gets $323.10, which checks out. He finally adds together the actual money from all the envelopes, once again arrives at $323.10, and is satisfied. Out of this money, he gives the young man $32.31, which is what the young man paid for the magazines. In addition, he gives him $16.15, which is one-half percent of the day's take from his area—his cut for making the collections. He averages $15 a day, for an hour's work a day. Well pleased, the young man goes home to his cold typewriter.

The sallow man now takes out a ledger and enters in it the amount of, and the number of, each bet according to the exact location where each bet was made. He adds his figures again to check his work and gets the correct total. By then, another collector has come in. The sallow man is one of six men at Novelty Amusement who each take in the receipts from five collectors. They work at this approximately from four until six o'clock. Each of them clears about $1,500 a day—resulting in a grand total of about $9,000 a day for the entire operation.

Ten-and-a-half percent of this money has already been paid out. The receivers each get one percent. Additional office salaries, rent, utilities, and so on eat up about 3½ percent more. When the sallow man stuffs the day's proceeds into a canvas sack and carries it back to the room marked "Bookkeeping," there's about 85 percent of it left. On an average day, this leaves about $7,700. Ten percent more is deducted almost immediately and put into envelopes which are delivered to law officers and other local authorities. Twenty-five percent is retained by the local organization and split among its chief personnel; the remaining 50 percent is shipped weekly to Chicago—the national organization's piece of the pie. In an average six-day week, this half of the pie comes to better than $25,000. Each day's cut is put in the safe in the bookkeeping room, and, on Saturday nights, two armed men carry the cash in a briefcase to Chicago by plane. For security, one of the armed men is from the local organization and one is from the national organization.

On this Saturday, there was $27,549, earmarked for Chicago, in the safe. In addition there was the $20,000 kept as a cash reserve—on the unlikely chance that, someday, there might be a run on a winning number, or for additional greasing when and if necessary, or for whatever unforeseeable emergency might arise. And further, there was $13,774.50, in the safe, which represents the week's 25 percent cut for the local organization to be split on Monday. The total in the safe was $61,323.50. Including the dime.

At six-fifteen, on this Saturday, a late mailman with a bulging bag walked into the Kenilworth Building, chatted with the elevator operator about special-delivery packages, and rode up to the ninth floor. He then took the fire stairs down to the seventh floor. A couple of minutes after he entered the building, two well-dressed men with briefcases, looking like insurance salesmen, walked into the building and rode up to the sixth floor. The elevator operator was a bit puzzled—it was Saturday and after six o'clock—that there was so much activity going on, but he brought the elevator back to the first floor, he found two bearded young men with trombone cases waiting for him. One of them said, "Hey, Pops. What floor's Associated Talent?"

"Tenth floor, but I think they all went home."

"They better not had, man. They called us over special. Weekend gig, man."

The elevator operator carried them up to the tenth floor.

On the seventh floor, down the hall from Novelty Amusement, the mailman was talking to the two apparent insurance agents about people who address their mail incorrectly. A few minutes later, the two trombone players emerged from the stairwell onto the seventh floor, joined the other three men, and the mailman looked at his watch. "We've got fifteen minutes," he said.

They all reached into the mailbag and came up with white handkerchiefs, which they tied over their faces like bandits.

Then, from the sack, they pulled two stubby shotguns with barrels sawed off back nearly to the stocks. The trombone players opened their trombone cases and produced partially assembled Schmeissers—burp guns with folding stocks. They put these together rapidly and snapped in clips.

The mailman said, "All right. Give me one minute."

He opened the door to Novelty Amusement and went inside. The other four men waited outside, one of the trombone players studying his watch intently. All the other offices on that floor were closed by that time. The collectors had all been and gone at Novelty Amusement, and the couriers weren't due for half an hour yet, so it was unlikely that the party would be interrupted.

The mailman walked into Novelty Amusement looking mild and baffled. He had a thick moustache, black edged with gray, and very thick glasses. He went over to the receptionist's desk. "I'm sorry, Miss, but I can't find this company. Do you know where Associated Removals is?"

The receptionist shook her head. "I never heard of it."

"Well, maybe that isn't it. The writing on the package label is terrible. Here, you take a look at it—" He came wandering around the desk. "—maybe it says something else and I'm reading it wrong."

The receptionist knew that no one was supposed to come behind the desk. If anyone tried to without permission, she was to push the button on the floor under her desk. But this time, she didn't even think of the button. She reached, instead, for the package. Suddenly, the mailman grabbed her wrist, yanked her from the chair, and hurled her into a corner. She landed heavily on her side, knocking her head against the wall. When she looked up dazed, the mailman had an automatic trained on her. "Can you scream louder than this gun?" he said in a low voice.

She stared at the gun. She couldn't have screamed if she'd wanted to. She couldn't even breathe.

The outer door opened and the four men came in, two carrying shotguns, and two machine guns. The girl couldn't believe it—it was like something in the movies. Gangsters carried machine guns back in 1930. There was no such thing as a machine gun in real life. Machine guns and Walt Disney mice—all make-believe.

The mailman put his gun away under his coat, and removed the mailbag from his shoulder. He took cord from the mail sack and tied the receptionist's hands and feet. She gaped at him unbelievingly as he tightened the knots. They were in the wrong office, she thought. It must be a television show shooting scenes on location—they must have wanted the office next door and these men had come into the wrong place. It must be a mistake.

The mailman gagged her with a spare handkerchief as one of the other men brought the two musical instrument cases and two briefcases in from the outside hall. The mailman took the briefcases. The men with the machine guns led the way. They all walked down the inner hall and stopped at the door next to the bookkeeping room. The mailman opened the door, and all five of them boiled into the room.

This was the room where the alarm buzzer would have rung if the receptionist had remembered to ring. Four men in brown uniforms wearing pistols and Sam Browne belts were sitting at a table playing poker. They jumped up when the door burst open—then they all froze. They believed in machine guns.

The mailman told them to lie on the floor, faces down, and they did so immediately. He used their ties to bind their hands, their belts to bind their feet. He tore strips from their shirts to gag them. Then the five men went back to the hall. One of the trombone players walked back to the receptionist's office and sat down at the desk, cradling the machine gun in his lap and guarding the door. The other trombone player stood at the far end of the hall, watching the closed doors that lined it. The phoney mailman and the insurance salesmen with their shotguns walked into the bookkeeping room.

There was only one man there, the chief accountant. He was standing by the window, smoking a cigarette, waiting for the couriers. He turned when the door opened, saw the three men coming in, and the cigarette dropped from his fingers. He raised his hands over his head. He was a C.P.A., a husband and father, forty-seven, medium height, somewhat paunchy, and not prepared to argue with sawed-off shotguns.

The mailman said, "Open the safe."

"I don't know the combination." He said it quickly, the first thing that came to his mind.

The mailman walked over and slapped his face with his open hand. "Don't waste my time."

"I really don't! I really don't!"

"All right, take off your shoes." The mailman took a penknife from his pocket and opened it.

The accountant stared at the penknife. "What are you going to do?"

"Every time I ask you to open that safe and you say no, I cut off one toe. You already owe me one. Take off your shoes."

"Wait! Wait, please! I'm not lying, I——"

He gestured to one of his men. "Take his shoes off."

One of the insurance salesmen came over, grabbed the accountant by the shirtfront, and dropped him into a chair. He stooped to grab the accountant's right foot.

The accountant shouted, "I'll do it! Don't! I'll do it!"

"You do it in under a minute, you don't lose any toes."

The accountant hurried to the safe. It was a big steel box, four feet high, three feet wide, three feet deep. He worked the combination hurriedly, but was so nervous he did it wrong the first time. He tried again, got it that time, and the safe opened.

While the mailman tied and gagged the accountant, the other two loaded the money from the safe into the briefcases. Then they went out into the hall where the trombone player joined them, and they walked to the receptionist's desk. They packed the burp guns into the trombone cases and the shotguns away in the mailbag. Once they were out in the outer hall, they removed their handkerchief-masks and shoved them into the mailbag.

Then they all went to the stairs. The insurance salesmen

went down to the sixth floor, the mailman to the ninth floor, the trombone players to the tenth floor. They rang for the elevator operator at almost the same time. He seemed pleased that the people he'd taken up separately would all be coming down together. Saved him two trips.

The trombone players got on first, and told the elevator operator they'd managed to get the gig for the weekend. One floor down, the mailman got on and said some idiot had mailed a special delivery package to the wrong address. Three floors lower, the insurance salesmen got on and discussed profit percentages with each other. The five men left the elevator and the building together. The mailman turned to the right and walked slowly off down the street. The trombone players stood in front of the building, lit cigarettes, and chatted together about their gig. The insurance salesmen went into the parking lot and got their car. When they came out of the lot, the trombone players sauntered over and slid into the back seat. The driver turned to the right, and, half a block further, stopped long enough for the mailman to climb aboard.

Forty minutes later, at a motel, the trombone players removed their beards, the mailman removed his glasses and moustache, and all five men washed the color rinse out of their hair. Then they got pencils and paper and split $61,323 five ways. They'd left five dimes in the safe. One of them was our lady's dime.

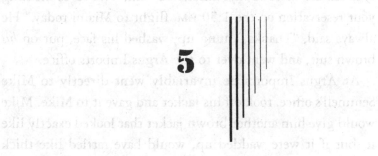

5

The same day and seven hundred miles to the east—

Once a month, Eric LaRenne put on a brown suit with $75,000 in cash sewn into the jacket lining and took a plane ride. They'd picked him for the job in the first place because he was in the Outfit anyway, in the right city, and was trustworthy. Besides he wore a size 36 short. This last attribute was most important, because the man at the other end wore a 36 short, too.

The man at the other end was Marv Hanks, and he had the same excellent qualities as Eric LaRenne. Once a month, he got a telegram—always on the same day that Eric LaRenne got his monthly phone call up north. The telegram always read: *"Mother sick. Must postpone visit. Effie."* On the day he received the telegram, Marv would put on his brown suit and go out to the airport to meet the 5:20 plane from the north.

The day chosen for Eric LaRenne's plane ride always began

the same way—with an early morning telephone call. Usually it came around nine o'clock, and, usually, it woke him up. A cool female voice always informed him, "We're confirming your reservation on the 1:50 P.M. flight to Miami today." He always said, "Thanks," hung up, washed his face, put on *his* brown suit, and went over to the Argus Imports office.

At Argus Imports he invariably went directly to Mike Semmell's office, took off his jacket and gave it to Mike. Mike would give him another brown jacket that looked exactly like it, but if it were wadded up, would have rattled like thick paper. LaRenne would put on the coat, leave the office, have a late breakfast, and go out to the airport to catch his plane. It was not a through flight; there was a change-over at approximately midpoint with a forty-minute wait. LaRenne always went all the way to Miami and spent a day or two there, but after the change-over his job was finished.

The way it worked, Hanks would be out at the airport when LaRenne's plane arrived. LaRenne would get off and go into the terminal to sit down for the forty-minute wait. At some point during the forty minutes, he and Hanks would switch jackets somewhere in the terminal building—perhaps in the luncheonette, or in the men's room, or out on the observation platform—wherever Hanks decided was best. Then LaRenne would get on the new plane and go on down to Miami. Hanks would take a cab back into town to Winkle's Custom House Trucking and go directly into Mr. Winkle's office. There he would take off LaRenne's suit coat and give it to Fred; Fred would give him another suit coat, and he would go home. In the pocket of the coat he wore home there would be an envelope containing a twenty-dollar bill and a five-dollar bill—his pay.

So there were four brown suit coats in the operation, all exactly alike, and that was the way the money was delivered. The heroin was sent back up some other way that neither LaRenne nor Hanks knew anything about. They didn't have to know about it, so they didn't know about it. All they knew was their own part, how to transfer the cash.

Four years before, LaRenne had fallen ill with appendicitis followed by pneumonia, and was unavailable for courier work for three months, so the Outfit had had to get someone else to take over the route. They'd chosen Artie Strand, primarily because he was a 36 short, and for three months he'd made the trips to Miami. It was necessary to have someone take over the route because it was a cash-before-delivery operation; if no money went down, no heroin came back up. A year and a half after LaRenne had recovered and gone back to work, the Outfit discovered that Artie Strand was unreliable and retired him with flowers. What they didn't know was that it was too late. He'd already shot his mouth off once too often.

Artie Strand was married, and his wife's brother was a stock-car racer named Fred Parnell. Parnell was also a driver in operations with people like Parker, Jacko, Handy McKay, and he was considered one of the best in the business. He never got nervous and stalled the engine, or picked the second-best route away from the hit. So he was called two or three times a year, from all over the country, to drive cars for jobs.

Because Strand was a loudmouth, Parnell knew what he did for a living, who his co-workers were, how much he took in a week, and everything else about him. Parnell never talked except to his cars, so Strand didn't know anything at all about Parnell. However, he guessed that Parnell skated over on the wrong side of the fence from time to time because Parnell spent more than he ever earned on the race tracks. So Strand figured they were not only brothers-in-law, but brothers under the skin, and that made it all right for him to shoot off his mouth.

One night, when Parnell was visiting his sister and they were all loaded on beer, Strand said, "You know what? You know what? If I ever need run-out money—you know what? I know right where to get it, you know that? *Right* where to get it. Seventy-five grand." He snapped his fingers. "Like that." This happened about two months after Eric LaRenne was back on the courier job again.

Naturally, Parnell started listening when he heard Strand talking about $75,000. Then Strand spilled the whole setup—the brown jackets, the pickup at Argus Imports, the plane ride, the stopover, and the switcheroo. Parnell listened, then asked one or two questions. He learned that the courier job—at least for the three months Strand had done it—had always taken place within the first week of the month. If the Outfit had men covering him at either airport to be sure he wasn't tapped, he, Strand, had never seen them. The amount was always the same—seventy-five grand—it never varied by a nickel.

Parnell was only a driver, and was afraid to hit the Outfit anyway so he just filed the information away in his head for a rainy day. Then, a little more than a year later, Strand fell off an elevated subway platform and died, so even if Parnell did pull the job there wouldn't be any way for the Outfit to trace the leak.

Then Parnell got the go-ahead letter from Parker. He'd worked with Parker three times, the last time five years ago, and got along with him better than with most. Nevertheless, he felt no particular kinship with Parker nor any responsibility toward him. He would have ignored the letter if it hadn't been for his sister's late husband.

But Strand had given him a setup and Parker had given him a reason to use it. With $75,000 he could build his own car again and take it to France and Italy the next summer for the races. All of his earnings from the jobs with Parker, Jacko, Handy McKay, and the rest of them went into his racers, which is why he could never save enough to quit. Besides, he didn't want to retire, not from either of his occupations, because he enjoyed them both in the same way.

Seventy-five grand.

He thought at first about doing the job himself. It could be a one-man operation with no trouble at all, but, when he thought it over, he changed his mind. He wasn't a heavy, he was a driver. So he got in touch with a heavy he knew, Kobler, and gave him the details of the score. Kobler agreed to come in, and they worked out the cut. Parnell would get 25 percent for fingering the job, Kobler would get 50 percent for pulling it off, and Parnell would get another 25 percent for driving the getaway car. Kobler hadn't liked the idea of giving Parnell 50 percent of the take without Parnell doing a 50 percent job like actually running the operation with him, but he didn't mind at all paying out 25 percent to the finger and 25 percent to the driver. Who cared if it was the same man both times? So they came to an agreement on the last day of the month.

Each moved out of his apartment. Parnell moved out of town altogether—down to the stopover city, where he found a furnished room three traffic lights from the airport, a distance of 2.6 miles. He sent the address to Kobler, whose move had taken him only across town to the apartment building facing the one where Eric LaRenne lived. Kobler had found out what Eric LaRenne looked like, and now spent every morning staring out the window at the street, waiting for LaRenne to emerge wearing a brown suit. LeRenne usually wore gray pants and a flannel shirt, so there'd be no question when the day of the job came along.

It came on a Tuesday, the fifth. Kobler watched LaRenne appear, wearing a brown suit, turn left, and then right at the corner at the far end of the street. As soon as LaRenne was out of sight, Kobler made his phone calls. His first call was to the airline, reconfirming Robert Southwell's seat on the 1:50 P.M. flight, for Miami. He had reserved a seat on the 1:50 flight for every day up until the tenth, using a different alias for each day, to be sure he would get on the flight with LaRenne. The girl confirmed Robert Southwell's reservation. He thanked her and broke the connection. Then he called Western Union and sent a telegram to Parnell: *"Arriving airport 5:20. Southwell."*

Kobler got dressed and packed his suitcase and briefcase. The suitcase had clothing and toilet gear in it; the briefcase contained a Ruger Blackhawk .357 Magnum revolver loaded with .38 Short Colt cartridges. Unlike most men in the business, Kobler didn't get rid of his gun after each operation and order a new one for the next job. He'd had the Blackhawk since 1955, when they had first come on the market, and he intended to keep it until he was forced to shoot somebody with it—which hadn't yet happened. When it did, he'd get another gun.

He was at the airport half an hour before take-off. He picked up his ticket, checked his suitcase through, but elected to carry his briefcase on board with him. Then he got in line directly behind LaRenne. Fortunately, the flight was a fairly full and there was nothing odd about Kobler sitting down next to LaRenne. He took out a magazine as soon as he sat down to keep LaRenne from starting a conversation with him. After the plane took off, Kobler dozed for a while, the briefcase lying on his lap. He was a big, meaty man with a blunt face and short, black hair. He looked like an ex-prizefighter who was now regional sales manager for a beer company.

Passengers usually look out the windows when a plane is landing. Kobler apparently woke up as the plane was landing and LaRenne was gazing out the window. So was everybody

else on the plane, except two or three businessmen who were
still reading their newspapers.

Kobler opened his briefcase, poked LaRenne on the arm.
"Look at this."

LaRenne turned, saw the open briefcase.

Kobler said, "Look inside."

LaRenne leaned forward and looked inside. When he saw
the Blackhawk he lunged back in his seat and stared at Kobler
goggle-eyed.

"Take it easy, LaRenne. I wasn't supposed to tip myself to
you before this, just in case." Kobler's voice was soft and easy.

"In case?" LaRenne was almost panicking, but was instinc-
tively keeping his voice as soft as Kobler's. "In case of what?"

"In case Hanks had a confederate anywhere around."

"Hanks?" It didn't make any sense to LaRenne that this
perfect stranger would know his name and know Hanks'
name, and whenever something didn't make any sense to
LaRenne he automatically looked as though the whole thing
was a wrong number. "I don't know what you're talking
about."

Kobler leaned close. "The seventy-five G's," he whispered.
"In the coat."

"*What?*"

"Keep it down!"

"Jesus Christ!" whispered LaRenne. "Who the hell *are*
you?"

The plane's wheels scraped the runway, bounced away,
scraped again. LaRenne and Kobler jounced against their

safety belts. When the plane calmed down, Kobler said, "I'm
your bodyguard. We just found out that Hanks is figuring on
walking off with the payment."

"He'd be crazy! They'd get him in a month!"

LaRenne had thought, more than once, of walking off with
the money, but had given the idea up because he knew the
Outfit would look for him until they found him, and they
would surely find him. Now he was mad when he heard that
Hanks had been thinking the same thing, and was even planning on *doing* it. It was as though he'd been cheated, as
though Hanks had stolen his idea and was getting the credit
for something that should have been his.

"Listen to me," said Kobler. "We only got a minute. I
would of told you before, but I fell asleep. You and me, we by-
pass Hanks. There'll be a car waiting for us. This time, you
bring the cash all the way. Next time, there'll be a replace-
ment for Hanks. You'll probably meet the new man this afternoon."

"But—I'm supposed to go all the way to Miami!"

"You'll get back in time. You've got forty minutes."

"But—"

"They couldn't tell you before you took off, can't you see
that? They don't know if there's anybody with Hanks or not."
The plane had stopped and people were standing up and
starting to walk down the aisle. Kobler whispered rapidly,
"You're not supposed to take my word for it. When we get in
the terminal, go over to Hanks and stall him. Then call the
boss and check if I'm on the level or not. You're not supposed

to take my word for it. But, just remember, if Hanks tries anything you give me this high sign. Got it?"

"I don't know," said LaRenne.

"Come on, let's get off the plane."

They were the last two passengers off. Out of the side of his mouth, Kobler said, "Act like you're not with me. If you see Hanks, signal him to wait a minute, then go straight to the phone booths and call the boss. Got it?"

"All right—all right."

LaRenne couldn't be sure if Kobler was on the up and up or not. He'd never seen Kobler around before, but that didn't mean anything. And what could happen to him in the terminal? He'd stall Hanks and make the phone call. If the call proved Kobler a liar, then LaRenne could signal Hanks for help. Anyway, LaRenne already believed that Hanks was planning to walk off with the money. Hadn't he thought about doing the same thing himself?

They walked into the terminal, Kobler one step behind LaRenne. LaRenne saw Hanks strolling across the terminal floor toward the luncheonette. LaRenne nodded briefly but kept walking away from the luncheonette at an angle. Hanks stopped and frowned, and LaRenne motioned with his head for Hanks to go on, trying to get the idea across that Hanks should wait a minute—that he should go on into the luncheonette and wait a minute. Hanks started walking again, but very slowly, watching LaRenne with a puzzled frown on his face.

Kobler hadn't known what Hanks looked like, but by following LaRenne's signals he spotted the frowning, puzzled man in the brown suit. He murmured to LaRenne, "I'll keep him busy. Hurry up with the call." Then he veered away from LaRenne and went over to talk to Hanks.

Hanks saw him coming, and looked more puzzled than ever, and also a little alarmed. He started angling away from Kobler, not wanting to talk with him, but Kobler caught up with him and asked, "Where's the others?"

"What? You got the wrong man, friend."

"You're Hanks, aren't you?"

Hanks debated denying it. Was this guy law or what?

Kobler hurried on. "Where's the others, god damn it? You want him to get away?"

"What? Who?"

"LaRenne! Didn't you people get the telegram?"

"What telegram?"

"Oh, for God's sake!" exclaimed Kobler. "LaRenne's figuring to walk off with the seventy-five G's. We just found out about it. I barely got on the same plane with him. He doesn't know me, see, he's never seen me around. Where the hell's he gone?"

Automatically, Hanks answered, "Back by the phone booths."

"Yeah. We figured he had somebody with him. Are there any more phone booths around here?"

"Listen," said Hanks. Things were going too fast for him. He'd thought of walking off with seventy-five G's lots of times, but he'd never had the guts to try it. He couldn't get used to the idea that maybe somebody else *did* have the guts. He was so shaken, he couldn't get his mental balance back.

And Kobler wouldn't give him the chance. "Phone booths, dammit!"

"Yeah, over there by the lockers. But—"

"No time! I don't want him to see you phoning nobody. Go over there to those other booths and call your boss and see didn't the telegram get there yet. Tell him to send two or three boys out here. We don't know who's with LaRenne or how many, and I'm not sure I can handle it by myself. Get going!"

"But—"

"I can't lose LaRenne!" said Kobler, and hurried away.

Hanks didn't know what to do. But LaRenne was acting funny, and the big guy had given him a reason for it, so he did what the big guy told him to do. He hurried across the echoing floor toward the other bank of phone booths on the far side of the terminal by the baggage lockers.

Kobler meanwhile went after LaRenne. He had disappeared into a double rank of phone booths. If you stood between the ranks, you couldn't be seen from the terminal proper. There were three people besides LaRenne closeted in booths, all of them talking like mad and paying no attention to the outside world. Kobler took out the Blackhawk, held it by the barrel and opened the door of LaRenne's phone booth. He clipped LaRenne with the gun butt just as the operator finally made the connection with Argus Imports.

A tinny voice sounded. "Hello?"

Kobler put the phone back on its hook, and stripped off LaRenne's coat. He stuffed coat and gun into the briefcase, closed it, and shut the phone-booth door. He walked over to the self-service baggage counter where the baggage from his flight was just coming in. He stood with his back to the terminal and when his bag was put on the counter, he picked it up and headed toward the exit to the parking lot. He was just going through the electric-eye doors when Hanks came running from the phone booths at the far end. He knew something was wrong, and it probably wasn't wrong with LaRenne. But he was staring at the phone booths far ahead of him, so he didn't see Kobler going out.

Kobler walked over to the parking lot where Parnell was sitting in a year-old Mercury station wagon with the engine idling. Kobler put the suitcase and briefcase in the back, got in front next to Parnell, and they drove back to Parnell's furnished room, where they split the coat up the back and the take down the middle.

Parnell caught a plane later that evening for New Mexico to start work on his new racer.

6

The next day, and four hundred miles to the south—

From the gas station, you could see the stands around the race track. Maury sat in the gas-station office, his feet up on the desk, and looked out the window past the pumps, and beyond the highway, to the stands which were topped by waving pennants. He sat there and waited for the phone not to ring. Every day during racing season, he spent his afternoons in the gas station, waiting for the phone not to ring, and most days it didn't.

But, every once in a while, it would and Willy, who ran the station, would pick it up and then turn to Maury and say, "It's for you." And Maury would have to run to the track. Maury didn't like to run, not to the track or anywhere. But God help him he should some day *walk* to the track and, as a result, get there too late to make the bet. On the days when the phone rang and Willy told him it was for him, Maury would jump

up and run over to the phone, crying, "Open the safe! Open
the safe! Don't just stand there!" And he'd be panting already,
even before making the run to the track, as he'd take the receiver, identify himself, and hear the voice at the other end
say, "Three on Mister Whisker."

"Three on Mister Whisker," Maury would repeat. Then the
party at the other end would cut him off. Maury would slam
the receiver, turn to Willy, and shout, "Isn't that damn safe
open yet?"

Willy would ask, "How much, Maury? Take it easy for
Christ's sake, Maury. How much?"

And Maury would say, "Three."

Then Willy would hand him $3,000 in hundred-dollar
bills, thirty hundred-dollar bills, and he would stuff them
into his pockets and run for the track. It would seem like forever getting through the gate, then he would be at the hundred-
dollar WIN window, and he'd say, "Three thousand on Mister
Whisker."

The clerk at the hundred-dollar WIN window would smile
and say, "Hello, Maury. Big play on that one, huh?" And he'd
take Maury's thirty hundred-dollar bills and give him thirty
tickets on the nose of Mister Whisker.

Maury could then relax for a few minutes. He could go
some place to watch the race, or just sit down and get his
breath back, until the particular race on which he bet was
over. If Mister Whisker came in, he'd go back and collect on
his thirty tickets. If Mister Whisker lost, he'd carry the thirty
tickets back to the gas station, put them in an envelope, and

mail them off to the commission house, so they'd know he actually had bet the three grand and not just pocketed it.

He'd thought sometimes of *not* betting the money, of sticking it in his pocket and waiting for the horse to lose. He could scrounge up enough tickets that other people had thrown away to make up the amount he should have bet. But most losers got their revenge by ripping the tickets up first. Besides, what if the horse won? If the horse won, and Maury hadn't had the money on it, he wouldn't be able to go back to the gas station with the winnings. And if that happened, God help him. So he took his fifty a week for sitting in the gas station and hoping the phone wouldn't ring, and every once in a while he ran across the highway with his pockets full of thousands of dollars that he knew better than to try to keep.

He'd gotten the job from his brother-in-law, his wife's brother, who was a big shot. Maury was a little shot and always would be. His brother-in-law had got him the job because otherwise Maury might not have been able to support his family, and, in that case, Maury's brother-in-law would have to. And the brother-in-law had made it clear this was one job, *the* one job in Maury's life, that Maury did not want to get himself fired from. "If you screw this up, Maury, there's nothing I can do for you. My sister will be a widow."

It was a hell of a responsibility, and it terrified Maury. That was why he spent every afternoon hoping the phone wouldn't ring.

What Maury was, he was the lay-off man. The occasional phone order he got began a long, tortuous distance away from him. It could begin with your corner bookie. Normally, your corner bookie likes to cover all his bets himself, because then he can keep all the money bet on losers. But, every so often there's a run on a horse—there's so much money bet on a particular horse running with high odds that if that horse came in, it would cost your corner bookie his shirt to pay off. Your corner bookie is a gambler, but he isn't crazy. So he calls one of the big bookies, in New York or Chicago or Miami, and lays off part of the one bet on that horse. If the horse doesn't come in, he's lost the money he laid off to the big bookie. But if the horse does come in, he'll have the money to cover the winnings and he can pay off his betters.

Just as the small-time bookie sometimes has to lay off an excess of bets on a horse, the big bookie sometimes has to do the same thing. Mister Whisker, say, is running at 12 to 1, which means a $24 pay-off on every $2 bet. A number of corner bookies have been getting runs on Mister Whisker, and have laid off part of the money with a big bookie. Not only that, but a number of the big bookie's regular customers are also betting heavily on Mister Whisker. So the big bookie calls a commission house in St. Louis or Cincinnati or Chicago, and he, in turn, lays off some of his bets.

After the commission house, there's no place left to lay off bets. Except at the race track itself. So the commission house, if necessary, does *its* laying-off right at the track. This system has a double advantage for the commission house. Not only does it cover the commission house bets, but a large win bet shortly before post time may also lower the odds at the track so that a horse which was paying 24 to 2 before the commission house placed its bet through a lay-off man at the track may actually end up paying only 10 to 2.

But although the commission house gains an additional advantage from a lay-off bet at the track, it is faced with an additional physical problem in making the bet. The corner bookie can phone the big bookie. The big bookie can phone the commission house. But the commission house can't phone the race track.

So the commission house does the next best thing. It hires a man to stand by near a telephone close to the race track every afternoon for the entire racing season. When the commission house wants to place a bet, it calls the man it has hired and tells him how much to bet on which horse. Then the lay-off man races over to the track and makes the bet personally.

There's only one rub. In order for the man to be able to make large bets when required, he must have large amounts of money handy. In the safe in the gas-station office, for instance, there was always a fund of between $30,000 and $50,000. When the fund dropped below thirty, it was replenished by a courier from the commission house. If a lay-off bet turned out to be a winner, any money won that brought the fund over $50,000 was immediately returned to the commission house.

That afternoon, when the phone rang at twenty minutes past two and Maury felt the panic wings flutter in his stomach, there was $42,000 in the safe.

*   *   *

Salsa had been sitting here in the car at the same spot every afternoon since he'd gotten Parker's goading letter, watching the gas station through his binoculars. He was beginning to lose patience. It was now Wednesday. He would wait it out till the end of the week. If there wasn't any action by then, he'd give it up.

Salsa was a tall, smooth-muscled man of thirty-seven, an illegal immigrant, whose youth had been thrown away on a passionate concern for a brand of politics currently in strong disfavor in the United States. In his middle twenties, he had suddenly awakened to the Truth of Self-interest, which he now realized was a far more important and valid Truth than any Political Truth ever invented. He further realized this was the hidden Truth upon which most of the leaders he had blindly followed based their actions. They had claimed to be struggling selflessly for a better world and Salsa had been young enough to believe them and to try to help them actively. He had actually been struggling selflessly for a better world until he had realized that most of the men he'd been following were struggling mainly for a world which would be better for themselves. From then on, when faced by a man who claimed he was struggling for a better world, Salsa invariably thought, "Better for *whom,* Brother?"

Just as, earlier, he had practiced what his leaders had preached, Salsa now began to emulate what they had practiced. But he was still too young, a little too brash and incautious in his methods, and it wasn't long before he had to flee. Several countries were unconscious hosts for him as he wandered about trying to find a place for himself in a suddenly topsy-turvy world. His youth and physical strength had helped and his good looks had helped even more. A number of women had taught him their native languages. He still spoke English with a slight British accent.

Eventually, Salsa discovered the gigolo's paradise, a luxury trans-Atlantic steamer. Staying aboard and not debarking at either end, he hid from authority when the ship was in port with the assistance of one or another of the shipping company's female employees. He spent three relaxed years on the same ship. There was good food; there were interesting companions. Clothing and pocket money could always be stolen, and there was inevitably a woman looking for a roommate, so he did not have to sleep on deck. But there was no permanence in that life, and no chance to accumulate the large sums which would enable him to retire to a life of ease. So, one day, he jumped ship in New York.

The United States was the obvious country for him—he'd been everywhere else in the world where Caucasians predominate, except Australia—but, because of the political foolishness of his youth and the undoubted moral turpitude of his present life, he didn't even bother applying for permission to enter the States. He already knew the answer. So he simply jumped ship, and waited to see what the New World had to offer.

It offered very little beyond dishwashing jobs and suspicious policemen until the day he ran into a fellow named Rico who was a professional thief. When Rico found out how much Salsa knew about guns, a part of his youthful political training, Salsa's new career was born. In the eight years since then, he had worked fourteen jobs, eight with Rico, two with Parker. The $17,000 that was his share of the first job he had been on bought him papers proving he was an American citizen, born in Baltimore, a veteran of the Korean War. He had a high school diploma, a driver's license, a Social Security card, an Army discharge form—everything he needed.

The money from the next two jobs went into setting up his new home on the north shore of Long Island. Salsa had purchased a large house, half-a-century old, on five-and-a-half acres with frontage on Long Island Sound. He owned a Ford Thunderbird and a Cadillac—he was a proud, chauvinistic citizen who wouldn't buy foreign cars or anything else made outside the good old U.S.A.—and a Chriscraft. His friends were mostly in television and advertising, and, among them, it was rumored that he had inherited wealth. He took a job whenever the larder was low, and the rest of the time was the proverbial playboy, the one the gentlemen's magazines describe so aptly.

It was a lucky accident that he found out about Maury and the money in the gas-station safe. He was aware of the lay-off system and how it worked, and knew that commission houses had men stationed around every major race track throughout the season. It just happened that he had stopped at that gas station—to feed the Thunderbird—one afternoon when a phone call had come for Maury.

Salsa had been driving south, in response to a party invitation which had been tendered him two days before by long-distance. While the attendant was pumping gas into the car, he went into the station office to buy cigarettes. There was a stocky, indolent man sitting at the desk, his feet up on the top. He was smoking a cigar. Salsa, discovering he didn't have any change, produced a dollar bill and asked the stocky man to change it. The stocky man said, "Jeez, Mac, I only got about eight cents change on me." He patted his pockets.

Salsa, confused, motioned at the cash register. "But surely—"

"I don't work here, Mac." Willy disliked and distrusted Maury, so he wouldn't let him open the cash register. "Willy! Hey! Guy here wants change."

Willy had come in from the work area and given him change. Salsa had gotten cigarettes from the machine and gone back to the car, wondering what the story was. A lazy man, feet up on the desk, but he didn't work there. Then Salsa looked up and noticed the stands further down on the other side of the highway. He asked the attendant at the gas pump, "What's that?"

"Race track."

And then Salsa had understood. He hadn't needed the rest of it. Just as he was pulling away, he saw Willy answer the phone in the office, then give the phone to the other man. He saw Willy crouch down near the safe, and nodded to himself. A lay-off man—with the capital in the gas-station safe. He filed the information away in the back of his mind for a very rainy day and drove on southward.

It would be an easy job to knock over, he thought, one man could do it alone. But Salsa had always worked on lays that somebody else had set up and planned, and he really didn't see himself as the kind of guy who could run a job from beginning to end. Besides, it was kind of an unwritten rule to leave syndicate operations alone. If he was ever really strapped for cash, he'd break that rule now that he knew about this setup, but until then he would forget it.

Salsa had forgotten till the letter came from Parker. Then he remembered, and smiled in anticipation. It would be a pleasure to knock that place over! His first solo job ought to be something easy, anyway.

He had driven down the same day and scouted the territory. There was an additional piece of luck he hadn't counted on, which came in handy. Next door to the gas station was a roadhouse which had burned down. The insides were gutted but the outer walls still stood. A lot of cheapskates who didn't want to pay at the race track parking lot left their cars in the parking lot beside the roadhouse, so Salsa simply parked his car among them. He could look straight across at the gas-station office and through the plate glass to the desk where the stocky man sat every afternoon. Salsa had the Thunderbird, decked out in false plates, and he'd worked out his getaway route. All he needed was for the stocky man to get a phone call.

That, he'd decided, was the only way to do it, to wait until a phone call came so the safe would already be open when he went in. In daylight, it would be too chancy to make somebody open the safe during working hours. Better let them open it first and *then* go in.

But over a week had gone by, and—nothing. Either he was wrong, which was unlikely, or the commission houses were having a long spell of clear weather. So he'd wait till the end of this week, and then the hell with it.

He was just repeating that to himself when he saw Willy go into the office and answer the telephone. It was a wall phone, near the door, and Salsa could see him standing there through the glass of the door. He saw Willy turn away and say something to the other man, saw the stocky man suddenly jump to his feet, and dash to take the phone. Before Willy had even turned toward the safe, Salsa had dropped the binoculars onto the seat and started the engine.

He didn't even have to go out onto the highway. A line of low scrub separated the black-top of the roadhouse parking lot from the black-top of the gas station. Salsa shot through the scrub driving one-handed while he slipped the mask on over his head with his other hand. It was a green Frankenstein mask he'd picked up in a five-and-ten. He clapped a hat on over the mask, and pulled the Thunderbird to a stop in front of the office. He jumped out of the car and strode in, pulling a gun from inside his jacket.

Maury was already off the phone. "Five on Flossie Billy. Five on Flossie Billy." Willy was counting five thousand out of the green metal box in the safe, hundred-dollar bills in stacks of ten bound with strips of paper.

"Move away from the safe. Shut it, and you're a dead man," Salsa said.

Maury spun around, and saw Frankenstein, with a hat and a gun. Willy was skittering back away from the safe, ashen-faced, and Maury screamed, "Shut it, Willy! Shut it!"

Then Frankenstein took a step toward him and swung the gun. It hit Maury's cheek and he fell backwards over the desk, landing in a heap on the floor. He saw things dizzily, through a red veil. He saw the masked man clout Willy with the gun. Then he saw him reach into the safe, stuff the hundreds back into the green metal box, shut it, and stand up with it tucked under his arm.

"Stay down," Frankenstein warned. "The first head that comes up, I'll shoot at through the window."

Then he backed out of the office and Maury heard a car engine start and the squeal of tires.

Willy was the first one up. He ran out of the station, leaving Maury there alone. Maury climbed up the desk and finally got his feet under him. He came staggering out, still feeling dizzy and terrified, and bumped into Willy, who was coming back in.

"I couldn't get a look at the damn plates," Willy said. "It was a cream Thunderbird, but I couldn't see the plates." He pushed past Maury. "Lemme get to the phone, will you?"

"Phone? Phone?"

"I got to call the police, dumbhead!"

"Police!" A new terror grabbed Maury. "Jesus Christ, Willy! You can't call the police!"

Willy stopped, his hand halfway to the phone. "Oh!" he said. He looked at Maury. "The son of a bitch gets away clean."

"I got to call my brother-in-law, Willy. Listen, you tell him. You tell him there wasn't nothing I could do. Right, Willy? You were right here, right? There wasn't nothing I could do."

"Yeah, yeah!" said Willy distractedly. There was a look of awe on his face. "He's away clean," he said. "The son of a bitch is away clean."

Maury dropped a dime into the phone, and dialed his brother-in-law's number. While the number was ringing, he had another thought, and turned a pale face to Willy. "Sweet Jesus!" he whispered. "What if Flossie Billy wins?"

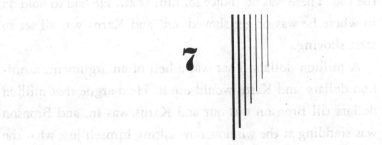

7

Bronson stood at one of the windows in his office, looking out at the night. Light spilled from other windows here and there along the façade of the house and illuminated the dark green lawn and the hedge separating lawn from sidewalk. The near curb was empty but, directly across the street, a blue Oldsmobile was parked. There was no traffic.

Twelve. Twelve robberies in five days. Over a million dollars gone, as though it had never been. Operations disrupted, customers upset, three Outfit employees dead. They couldn't take that kind of beating. For God's sake, a million dollars. *Nobody* could take a beating like that.

And now Karns, that bastard from the West Coast, wanting a meeting of the national committee, wanting to know how the hell Bronson had managed to get them all into this mess in the first place. Karns wanted Bronson's chair, and the only way a man ever moved up to another man's chair was if

the other man either moved up or got shoved off on his ass.
But in Bronson's case there was no up to move to—he was at
the top. There was no choice for him at all. He had to hold on
to where he was or get shoved out, and Karns was all set to
start shoving.

A million dollars. That was a hell of an argument, a million dollars, and Karns would use it. He'd argue that million
dollars till Bronson was out and Karns was in, and Bronson
was standing at the window now asking himself just what the
hell he planned to do about it.

If it was only Parker, it wouldn't be too bad. Go to the
meeting with Parker's head on a tray—that would shut
Karns' face. But it wasn't only Parker. Four robberies in one
day, scattered all over the country. It wasn't only Parker, it
was Parker and all his damn friends. It was people Bronson
had never heard of, people who were leaving banks and pay-
rolls and armored cars and postal trucks alone all of a sudden,
and hitting the Outfit instead. Hitting race tracks and casinos and lay-off bookies and numbers collectors. Waltzing
away with a million dollars in five days and giving that bastard Karns the opportunity he'd been waiting for since '56.

Bronson brooded. Hang it on Fairfax? Maybe that would
do it. The whole mess with Parker had started in New York,
in Fairfax's territory. Fairfax had met Parker, had talked with
him, had set up the trap which Parker had breezed through
when he'd been paid his lousy $45,000. So even though Fair-
fax had set up the trap at Bronson's order and Stern had been

sent South at Bronson's order, those arrangements could be sloughed over.

All right. Call the meeting Karns wanted. Throw Fairfax in Karns' lap. Then see what could be done about Parker. Square the beef with him or kill him, whichever seemed best. Kill him, if possible, otherwise, square things. Let Karns chew on Fairfax and the hell with them both. Bronson had never liked Fairfax much anyway.

And when things quieted down, move a few reliable people into the West Coast operation and gradually nudge Karns out.

So the whole thing was good in a way. It had brought Karns into the open, had let Bronson see which of the regional men he had to worry about as far as trying to take over was concerned. It was Karns—now he knew it. And he had also learned that none of the others was dangerous, because only Karns was trying to blame Bronson. So now he knew more than he'd known before. Besides that he could get rid of Fairfax, so maybe Parker was doing him a favor.

All over the house, rococo clocks struck eleven. Bronson grimaced at the muffled sounds. A cab stopped out front. Quill. Bronson had been up here waiting for him, but, now that Quill was actually coming up the walk, it didn't matter anymore. There were twelve robberies already, so how much did the first one matter? Furthermore, he'd just planned how to get everything straightened away.

Bronson watched Quill coming up the walk, and, beyond him, he noticed the blue Oldsmobile still parked across the street. It irritated him. This wasn't a street for blue Oldsmobiles. This was a street for Cadillacs, for Rolls-Royces and Bentleys, for Imperials and Continentals, and an occasional ancient gray Packard.

But the character of the street was changing, no denying it. He wondered if Willa would be wanting to sell the house soon, and who would buy it. A convent, maybe, or a school for retarded children. Half the houses along the street had already been turned into institutions. Bronson's neighbor to the left was now a school for the blind, his neighbor to the right a fraternal organization's headquarters with a small blue neon sign over the door. Neon! On a street like this! But streets like this were anachronisms. Today's rich were all Arthur Bronsons; they preferred red leather and chrome. The old mansions were too forbidding, and too heavily taxed; the foundation of society was being displaced by foundations.

The blue Olds was a sign of it. Someone working late at one of the institutions, no doubt. Bronson shrugged it out of his mind and went out to the hall to meet Quill, who had been let in by one of the bodyguards. Willa was already in bed. They had played Russian bank together that afternoon, but it had only upset both of them. Bronson didn't really like Russian bank. He played it because he had to do something to relieve his boredom. He felt guilty about wanting to avoid Willa in her own home, and Russian bank was the game Willa liked to play. They didn't play for money or anything, just to see who would get high score and win, so it didn't do much to liven things up.

Bronson didn't know it, but Willa didn't care for card games at all, not Russian bank, or any other card game. She played because she knew her husband liked cards and because she wanted to keep him from getting too bored. Usually, when they played, she kept up a steady chatter of small talk, not because she wanted to, but because she thought the chitchat also would help to ease her husband's boredom. But, when he was worried about business, she knew he preferred silence, so that afternoon she had been silent.

Bronson had been glad Willa was quiet for once. On each of his rare visits home, they played Russian bank, and usually she talked her head off and nearly drove him crazy, but he didn't say anything about it because he didn't want to spoil her enjoyment. He was so seldom home anyway. That afternoon she had been silent, which was a relief, particularly since he kept losing.

Willa had tried not to win, because she knew it made her husband feel better if he won, but he hadn't been concentrating on the game at all so she kept winning despite herself. She wore an apologetic frown throughout the game because she couldn't keep from winning. She was keeping score, and she kept adding her score up wrong, to give herself less than she really had, but it didn't do any good. She just kept on winning until finally they quit by mutual consent. Bronson hadn't seen her since, except for a glimpse of her going by the office door on her way to bed, an hour ago.

He had to get out of this mausoleum soon. Willa was driving him crazy. When he was away from her, it was all right,

but when he was in the same house with her, he felt as though
he ought to make some effort to be friendly to her, and the
strain left his nerves ragged.

Well, at least he wouldn't have to introduce her to Quill.
Some sense of his being an interloper himself forced him to
introduce everybody who came in the house to see him to
Willa, including the bodyguards. At the same time, he knew
it was ridiculous to introduce your bodyguards to your wife as
though they'd come for a meeting of the gentlemen's auxil-
iary of the D.A.R. But she was in bed, as she'd been the first
time Quill had come, so, fortunately, he wouldn't have to present him this time either.

Bronson stood at the head of the stairs and watched Quill
come up. Quill was the new breed: He wore gray suits and
horn-rimmed glasses, he carried a briefcase, he looked like an
insurance adjustor, and if he ever did tote a gun, which was
unlikely, it would be a Berretta Minx.

"Hello, Mr. Bronson," Quill said, from the landing. He
started up the rest of the way. "A real mess, that Cockatoo situation." He could have *been* an insurance adjustor, the way he
talked.

*If he switches the briefcase to his left hand and tries to shake hands
with me,* Bronson thought savagely, *I'll kick him downstairs.*

But Quill shook hands only with clients or other adjustors,
not with employers. He reached the head of the stairs and
said, "Very nice house, Mr. Bronson. Really very fine."

"You said that last time."

"I must mean it, then."

"Yeah. Well, Quill, come on into the office."

Bronson led the way. Of course, this was necessary. What he'd been thinking a minute ago—that the talk with Quill was superfluous now—was wrong. The Club Cockatoo had been robbed, which should have been impossible. It was Quill's job to find out why it *had* been possible, so it would never be possible again. And after analyzing the Cockatoo problem, Quill would have to investigate the other eleven robberies as well. Something was wrong with the whole organization if they could be hit so easily. No matter what was done, with Parker, with Karns, with Fairfax, these other problems were real and had to be solved.

They went into the office. Bronson sat at his desk while Quill opened his briefcase and started producing masses of paper.

"I made a thorough investigation, Mr. Bronson," he said, "and I believe I have come to some conclusions which may startle you."

"Is that right?"

"Now—" Quill started to open one folded sheet of paper which he kept unfolding endlessly. It eventually turned out to be a large blueprint of the Club Cockatoo. "Now, in order for you to get the picture, to see *why* this happened, you'll have to see *how* it happened. May I?"

He wanted to spread the plan on the desk. Bronson grudgingly cleared space for it. Then Quill stood at his elbow, planted a finger on the blueprint and started talking. He had reconstructed the movements of the robbers from beginning to end, and he now described the robbery in detail, his finger tracing the path of the robbers in through the front door, through the maze of the plan and out again by the side door. Despite himself, Bronson got interested in the recital, and followed the operation, his eyes on the moving finger.

After his reconstruction of the robbery, Quill straightened up and went to the other side of the desk for his briefcase and the mass of papers.

"I have here," he said, "statements from virtually every Club Cockatoo employee. You can go through them later, I'll just give you the high spots now."

He put the mass of papers on the corner of the desk and ticked off the main facts on his fingers. "Number one: No one at the Club Cockatoo, from the manager on down, had ever considered the possibility of an armed robbery by experienced professionals. They were prepared for amateurs, who might come in waving guns and shouting, 'Stick 'em up,' or pass notes to the cashiers to put all the money in a canvas bag, that sort of thing, but they were not on guard, against intelligent professionals.

"Number two: No one at the Club Cockatoo, from the manager on down, had any idea what to do in case a successful robbery actually did take place. There was no organized plan, no procedure for this eventuality. As a result, the search for the robbers was undertaken exclusively by a limited number of Club Cockatoo employees, with no experience or instruction in this kind of activity. It wasn't until five hours after the robbery that the manager finally thought to call the local organization head for more capable assistance. By then, of course, it was too late. If the call had been made at once, there would have been fifty expert armed men on the robbers' trail within half an hour.

"Number three: No one at the Club Cockatoo, from the manager on down, was prepared to offer any real resistance to an armed robber. The attitude seems to be that the Outfit makes enough money to absorb a robbery or two, so there's no sense risking one's life.

"Number four: The employees of the Club Cockatoo all behaved as though they were employees of any ordinary lawful corporation, without the self-awareness of divorcement from society which should reasonably be a part of their make-up."

Bronson was lost by now, but he nodded anyway.

Quill held up four fingers. "So there are four things which set the club up," he said. "They didn't think they'd be robbed, they hadn't thought about what to do if they *were* robbed, none of them would risk being shot to protect the organization's money, and they didn't think of themselves as crooks. In a nutshell."

"Hold on." Bronson held up his own hand, fingers splayed like a traffic cop's. "What do you mean, they don't think they're crooks?"

"They *work* for a living. They have an employer; they pay income tax; they come under Social Security; they own their own homes and cars; they work in local industry. They know the corporation they work for engages in illegal activities, but they think what-the-hell, *every* corporation these days does, from tax-dodging through price-fixing to government bribing."

"What's that got to do with anything, Quill?" There was an undertone of warning in Bronson's voice. He thought of himself exactly as Quill had described it. He wasn't a *crook*. Bastards like Parker were crooks. Bronson thought of himself as a businessman. All right, he was a *criminal*, but everybody was more or less dishonest, particularly in business.

But if Quill noted Bronson's warning, he chose to ignore it. "They work for the Outfit, Mr. Bronson, for the *syndicate*. They're outside the law, outside society. And if they—" He stopped to marshal his thoughts. Finally, he went on. "Let us suppose, let us suppose there's a crap game going on in that park across the street. In the crap game there's two burglars, a mugger, a professional killer, and an arsonist. Now, let us suppose you—let us suppose *I* go over there with a gun to hold them up. What will happen?"

Bronson smiled grimly. "They'd tear your heart out," he said, enjoying the image.

"Of course. And why? Because they're *crooks*. They're outlaws, crooks. They don't think of themselves as part of society, they think of themselves as individuals, alone in a jungle. Therefore, they are always on the defensive, always ready to protect their own. They'll never call for the police, never put in a claim in their fire and theft insurance, never look to *society* to protect them or repay them or avenge them. Shouldn't people who work for the syndicate think the same way? But

they don't. The people at Club Cockatoo don't think of themselves as crooks at all, they think of themselves as average
working stiffs. Therefore, they let two robbers come in and
walk all over them. Whereas, if they thought of themselves as
do our hypothetical crapshooters in the park, they would have
torn those robbers' hearts out."

"You mean the Outfit's getting soft?"

Quill smiled, pleased with himself. "I mean the Outfit is
being civilized, is being absorbed into the culture. The organization is getting too highly organized."

"Is that right?" Bronson was no longer certain whether he
should be angry at Quill or agree with him. "What do we do
about it? You got any ideas?"

"I don't think anything *can* be done about it. If you managed to convince the employees of the Club Cockatoo that
they are crooks after all, nine out of ten of them would quit
on the spot and go get jobs some place else. They don't *want*
to be divorced from society." Quill smiled and spread his
hands. "A result of prosperity, I suppose. During the Depres-
sion, there was no such problem."

Bronson was tempted to ask *How would you know?* but he
kept his mouth shut, asking instead, "What else, then? Don't
you have any ideas at all?"

"Yes, I do." The lecture finished, Quill became brisk. "You
may have noticed, as I did, the one glaring weakness in the
Club Cockatoo's defense. That door from the men's room to
the cashiers' space."

"If they gotta go, they gotta go."

"Of course. In *pairs*. And there should always be an armed man at the door, on the cashiers' side."

Bronson glanced down at the blueprint. "Sure, why in hell didn't *they* think of that?"

"They did. Fifteen or twenty years ago, that was the rule. Cashiers went to the men's room in pairs. There was an armed man constantly on duty in the cashiers' space. But nothing ever happened, and over the years they grew lax. It slowed down the action to have two cashiers away at once so the armed man took to sitting in the office, where the safe was, and where he could chat with the manager."

"The goddamn fools!"

"Of course. Because a robbery had never been attempted, they no longer considered one a possibility." Quill shrugged. "Well, I think we may have learned from this."

"And the others?"

"I'd heard there'd been some more."

"Eleven more! I want you to check them out, just like you did this one."

"I imagine I'll find the same problems."

"You got any answers?"

"Suggestions only, Mr. Bronson. First, every organization operation which normally or occasionally has custody of large sums of money should be informed of these robberies, so they'll be reminded a hit *can* happen. Second, every operation should know whom to call so trained armed men can get on the job immediately in case a robbery *does* take place. Third, if a robbery occurs and is successful because of sloppiness among organization employees, such employees should be punished, perhaps by taking a cut in pay to help make up the loss."

"A cut in pay! What the hell do you think this is, a kindergarten?"

Quill smiled sadly. "Yes, Mr. Bronson, I'm afraid that's exactly what it is. If what I saw at the Club Cockatoo is an accurate sampling, most organization employees are simply average workers, as apathetic and uncommitted on questions of law and order as any of their neighbors. If General Electric threatened to kill any employee who did badly in his work, the workers would think somebody had gone crazy. They wouldn't believe it. A garnishee on their wages, they would believe. I'm not thinking now in terms of proper punishments or sufficient punishments, but *effective* punishments."

Bronson rubbed a hand across his face, feeling lost and confused. He was too far up the ladder; it had never occurred to him that the rank and file had turned into a bunch of nine-to-fivers. What the hell kind of world was this? Next thing, they'd be wanting a union. Or a guild. They probably thought of themselves as white collar workers. Sweet Jesus!

"All right," he said. "All right, Quill, that's good. You did a good job."

"There's more, Mr. Bronson."

"Yeah, I bet there is. Save it. Tomorrow morning. We'll go over it some more in the morning, and I'll give you the list of the other places that got hit."

"Yes, sir, Mr. Bronson."

"Yeah, good night."

Left alone, Bronson sat at his desk, brooding. What the hell had happened? He could remember the twenties, and it was nothing like this. Did anybody in the Outfit go around then with a briefcase full of statements?

"*We* were the Parkers then." He said it aloud, surprising and angering himself. He got up from the desk, went to the window, and looked out at the park, thinking of Quill's crapshooters. Were there any Outfit people in that game? A few, maybe, but just a few.

That bastard Parker belonged in that game. Bronson could see him now, getting out of that blue Olds over there and going into the park, not giving a damn about anybody. Hell, half the Outfit people wouldn't go *into* that park at night.

He wondered where Parker was, right this minute. He wondered if those four bodyguards were any damn good—they'd never had to show their stuff. He felt a slight chill in his spine.

When he turned away from the window, the hall door was open. There was a man standing there. Bronson had never seen him before in his life, but he knew right away it was Parker.

He wasn't even surprised.

FOUR

Four

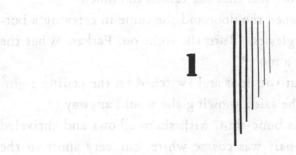

1

Two days after knocking over The Three Kings, Parker sat in his darkened room in the Green Glen Motel just north of Scranton and looked out the window at Route 6.

It was eight-thirty, Thursday night; Handy was due in half an hour.

He heard footsteps coming along the cement walk and leaned back, waiting for whoever it was to pass his window. But the footsteps stopped and there was a rapping at his door. Madge's voice called, "Parker? It's me." Parker shook his head and got to his feet. He'd have to talk to her.

Madge ran the Green Glen Motel. She was in her sixties now, one of the rare hookers who'd retired with money in the bank. Running this motel brought her a modest living, gave her something to do, and, indirectly, kept her connected with her original profession, for most of the units were rented by the hour. Because she could be trusted, her motel was also used sometimes as a meeting place by people in Parker's line of work. The only thing wrong with her was that she talked too much.

Parker opened the door and she came in carrying a bottle and two glasses. "Turn the light on, Parker. What the hell are you, a mole?"

Parker shut the door and switched on the ceiling light. "Sit down," he said, knowing she would anyway.

Madge was bone-thin, with sharp elbows and shriveled throat. Her hair was coarse white, cut very short in the Italian style. It was cold outside but she hadn't bothered to put on a coat for the walk from the office. She was wearing brand-new black wool slacks with shadow-sharp creases and a white blouse with large black buttons down the front. Triangular turquoise Indian earrings dangled from her ears, and black thonged sandals revealed her pale feet and scarlet toenails. Her eyebrows had been completely plucked, and redrawn in satanic, black lines. Her fingernails were long, curved, and blood red. But she wore no lipstick; her mouth was a pale scar in a thin deeply lined face.

She put the glasses down on the bureau and held up the bottle for Parker to see. Haig & Haig. "Just off the boat," she said, and laughed. She had gleaming white false teeth. Inside the young clothes was a young woman. Madge wouldn't let herself be old. It was 1920 and she was as young as the century—the Great War was over, Prohibition was in, money was everywhere. It was a grand thing at the very beginning of the Jazz Age to be alive and young and a high-priced whore. It would be 1920 around Madge till the day she dropped dead.

"You want ice?" she asked him. "I can go get some ice if you want."

"Never mind," said Parker. He wanted to get it over with, get the talking begun and done. Handy was due soon.

She splashed liquor into both glasses, handed him one, and said, "Happy times!"

He grunted. The liquor, when he tasted it, was warm and sour-sharp. He should have had her go for the ice.

She went over and sat on the bed. "What a sourpuss. I just can't get used to that new face, Parker. You know, I think it's even worse than the old one."

"Thanks." He went over and looked out the window again. When Handy got here, he'd have an excuse to throw Madge out.

"Did I tell you Marty Kabell was here last summer? He had some blonde with him, Christy or something. He had a mustache, too. . . ."

She talked away at his back as he stood looking out the window. She told him whom she'd seen in the last year, whom she'd heard about, where this one was now, what happened to that one. She was full of information. Some of the names she mentioned Parker didn't recognize, Madge thought all the people she knew also knew one another.

One big happy family. It was part of her still being twenty years old.

A car turned in from the highway and Parker interrupted her. "You got a customer."

"Ethel's minding the store." Ethel was a cow of a girl, about twenty-five, somewhat retarded. She lived at the hotel and worked for Madge, cleaning the units when they were vacated, sometimes taking over in the office. Where she'd come from and what connection she had with Madge, Parker neither knew nor cared. Some people thought she was Madge's daughter.

Madge kept talking. Every once in a while she'd pause or ask a question, and Parker would have to rouse himself and reply. Madge liked to talk too much, but she was valuable, and it was worthwhile to put up with her. Hers was the safest place in eastern Pennsylvania.

Ethel passed by the window, carrying a key, followed by a teen-age couple with their arms around each other's waists. The girl looked frightened; the boy looked intense. After a minute, Ethel came back alone, headed for the office. Behind Parker, Madge still talked. She was asking questions now, trying to store up more information on comings and goings to pass on to the next friend who stopped by. Parker answered in monosyllables: "In jail." "Out in California some place." "Dead."

At last another car pulled in from the highway. Parker finished the warm liquor and said no to a second drink. He half-listened to Madge, and half-listened for footsteps on the walk. He heard them and waited, and then there was a knock at the door.

Handy. But, just in case, he said to Madge, "Answer it for me, will you?"

"Sure. You in trouble, Parker?"

"No."

Madge shrugged, still in a good humor, and went over to open the door. "Hello, Handy! Come on in."

"What say, Madge?" Handy was tall and lean as a one-by-twelve, with knobby wrists, a bony face, and stiff, dark hair graying over the ears. He had a cigarette dangling from his mouth, and when he took it out it was badly lipped, brown tobacco showing through wet gray paper.

"It's real good to see you, Handy," said Madge. "Hold on, I'll get another glass."

Parker said, "Later on, Madge."

"Business," Madge replied. "It's always business with you, Parker." She put a hand on Handy's arm. "Come on over to the office later, we'll get drunk."

"Sure thing, Madge." Handy grinned, and held the door open for her. She went through and he closed the door and turned to Parker. "She's a good girl."

"She talks too much. How've you been?"

"So-so. Never any static on that armored car job. You read the papers on it?"

Parker shook his head. That was three months ago, he and Handy and two others had taken an armored car in New Jersey. If it wasn't for this Outfit thing, he'd still be in Florida, living on the take from that job. He and Handy had split it down the middle, because the other two had tried a cross and it hadn't worked for them.

"They never even got a beginning," Handy said. He went over to the bureau and crushed his cigarette in the ashtray. It sizzled. Then he pulled a box of small-sized wooden matches from his pocket, got one out, and stuck it in the corner of his mouth. Between cigarettes, he always sucked on a wooden match. He turned back to Parker and said, "You remember what I told you after that job? I told you it was my last one. I'm retiring."

Parker nodded. Handy quit after every job—he'd been doing it for ten years or more.

"I mean it this time," Handy told him, as though he knew what Parker was thinking. "I been up in Presque Isle, Maine. They got them an air force base up there, and I'm buying in on a diner, right across the road from the main gate. Open all night. I short-order a good egg when I put my mind to it, so I'll work the nights myself."

"Good luck."

"Damn right." Handy moved over and sat down on the edge of the bed. "I been in the business too long. I'm a lucky man, Parker. You, too. Both of us, too damn lucky. But there's no string goes on forever, and I figure mine's just about played out. I'll settle down in Presque Isle and short-order a few eggs and let the rest of the world go by." He nodded, and prodded at his teeth with the match.

Handy was wearing gray corduroy pants and a red-and-black hunting jacket. Parker looked at him and could imagine him running a diner, but, at the same time, he knew Handy would come back in whenever he was offered a seat in the game. All the diner meant was that Handy would be going back to the same place every time from now on. But he wouldn't be turning down any jobs that looked good. He'd driven down to see Parker knowing nothing of the reason for the summons, and his presence here was proof that he wouldn't be short-ordering eggs *every* night for the rest of his life.

Parker pulled the blind down over the window and crossed the room to sit in the easy chair by the bureau. "This isn't a job I called you about," he said. "Not the regular kind, anyway."

"What kind, then?"

Parker filled him in on what had happened, the killer who'd missed, the letters to the pros, taking care of Menner, and knocking over The Three Kings.

Handy listened to it all, poking at his teeth with the match, and when Parker was done he said, "I been thinking. Out of the people I know, there's at least eight'll be real happy to get that letter of yours. They'll go right out and do jobs they been thinking about all these years." He grinned and nodded. "This Bronson and his friend, I bet they're hurting right now."

"They'll hurt more." Parker lit a cigarette. "Anyway, I know where Bronson is. I'm going there."

"What else?"

"I could use a man beside me. I'm not in this one for the dough, so I'll give you the take from the poker game and The Three Kings. Forty-two hundred. Plus whatever we pick up in Bronson's house."

"I wasn't in on those two. Why give me the dough from them?"

"Make it worth your while. Bronson may not have much on him."

Handy shrugged. "Keep the dough, Parker. We known each other for years. We'll split the take from Bronson, and call the rest for old time's sake."

Parker frowned. He didn't like it that way. He said, "A split all the way, then. Twenty-one hundred for each of us, plus Bronson."

"Why?" Handy left the match in his mouth while he fumbled for another cigarette. "Why you want to give money away all of a sudden?"

"I'm not giving it away. I'm making it worth your while. You don't want to do a job for nothing."

Handy watched himself light the new cigarette. He leaned over to drop the match into an ashtray and then shrugged. "All right," he said. "A split all the way." He lipped the cigarette, then grinned and looked over at Parker. "I could use the money, anyway."

"For the diner."

"Sure, for the diner." Handy settled back on the bed, relaxing. "When do you want to go after this Bronson?"

"Early next week. By then, the Outfit'll have been hit a

few times. I want to be sure this guy Karns won't be in any hurry to cause trouble when he takes over."

"When do you want to go to Buffalo?"

"Tomorrow. We can use the time getting set up. How's your car? Hot?"

"Not a bit. Paid cash for it in Bangor. Absolutely legitimate."

"Same name as with the diner?"

"Sure. My own."

"We'll use mine then. To be on the safe side. It can't be traced back to me."

"It's a mace?"

"Yeah. I got it off Chemy, in Georgia. You know, the little guy with the brother?"

"Sure. It should be okay, then."

"It is."

"All right." Handy got to his feet. "I'm gonna stop in with Madge for a while. Come along?"

"Not tonight."

"See you in the morning, then."

Handy went out, and Parker switched off the light. He sat by the window, smoking, and looking out at the highway. Handy was troubling him. Buying a car, buying it legitimate. Buying into a diner, and planning to work in it. And being willing to come into a job for nothing out of sentimentality.

It was a bad sign when a man like Handy started owning things and started thinking he could afford friend-

ships. Possessions tie a man down and friendships blind
him. Parker owned nothing, the men he knew were just
that, the men he knew, not his friends and they owned
nothing. Sure, under the name Charles Willis he had pieces
of a few businesses here and there, but that was for tax reasons. He stayed away from those places, had nothing to do
with them, didn't try to get a nickel out of them. What
Handy was doing was something else again—buying
things to have them. And working with a man, not for a
profit, but because he *liked* him.

When a man like Handy started craving possessions and
friendships, it meant he was losing the leanness. It was a
bad sign.

2

Syracuse started flat, with used-car dealers and junkyards. Then came stucco bars and appliance stores in converted clapboard houses. It was late Friday afternoon, with rush hour and weekend traffic starting to overlap. Parker pushed the Olds through the traffic, making the best time he could. South Salina Street. The stores got taller and older, the traffic heavier, till they were downtown, where all the streets were one way the wrong way.

"I hate this city," Parker said.

"It's a city," Handy replied. "They're all like this."

"I hate them all, then. Except resort towns. Miami, Vegas, you don't run into this kind of thing."

"You're like me, you like a little town. You ever been to Presque Isle?"

"No."

"You should see the winters. Snow over your head."

"Sounds great."

Handy laughed. "I like it," he said. "We turn at the next corner. You make a right."

"It's one way the other way."

"Oh, yeah. Take the next right and circle around. I forgot about that one-way stuff."

The next corner was no good either. The cross street was one way, in the same direction as the block before it. Parker ran on down another block in time to get stopped by the traffic light. Women in heavy coats carrying clothing store boxes massed around the car in a herd. It wasn't December yet, but the Christmas decorations were up. A few Thanksgiving decorations were still up, too; nobody'd remembered to take them down.

The light turned green and Parker made the right. The next cross street still was one way the wrong way. "They got any one-way streets in Presque Isle?"

"Maybe one or two. You can live there all your life and not have to worry about it."

"Maybe I'll go there some day."

"Stop in the diner, I'll fry you an egg."

"Thanks."

The next street allowed them to go in the direction they wanted.

Handy said, "I'm sorry about this. I wish I knew somebody in Buffalo, then we could of just by-passed this town."

"It'd be the same in Buffalo."

"Yeah, but we'd *be* there."

"After you make the connection, we'll get up north of town by the thruway and stop in at a motel. I don't want to drive any more after this. We can get to Buffalo tomorrow and still have plenty of time."

"Okay, good. Park anywhere."

"Sure."

There weren't any parking spaces. They passed the building they wanted, and there still weren't any parking spaces. The curb for the last half-block to South Salina Street on the right was empty of cars, but lined with *No Parking* signs. Parker would have been willing to go around the block again, but to go around the block again, he'd have to go halfway around the city, so he pulled to the curb in the forbidden zone and shut off the engine. Let them give him a ticket. The car was a mace anyway. And he wouldn't have it more than a week or two. Once the job was done, he'd unload it, so let them copy down the license number in their little books and pile the tickets on the hood like snow.

They both got out of the car. Parker locked it, and they walked back down the block to the building they wanted, two tall men in hunting jackets and caps among the milling herd of short, stocky women with their arms full of packages.

It was an old building, with plaster walls painted a bad green. There were two elevators, but only one of them was running. Because it was nearly six o'clock, the old man who ran the one elevator was sitting on his stool with his coat on, waiting for the last few tenants to come down so he could go home. He frowned when he saw Parker and Handy, because he knew they'd be keeping one of the tenants past six o'clock.

"Everybody's gone home," he said, hoping they'd believe him and go away.

Handy had called earlier today, from Binghamton. "Our man's still here. Third floor we want."

Handy's man was Amos Klee, and on the directory between the elevators it said: AMOS KLEE, *Confidential Investigations*. Klee was a licensed, bonded private detective, but if he'd tried to make a living as a private detective in a city like this with an office in a building like this one he would have starved to death in a month. Klee had one priceless asset which paid his rent and kept him in spending money. That asset was his pistol permit. Plural. Pistol *permits*. The State of New York had given Amos Klee three pieces of paper each of which allowed him, for purposes of business, to own and to possess and to carry a pistol. Three pieces of paper, three pistols. Klee normally owned between fifty and a hundred pistols, but he never had more than three at a time where they might be noticed.

Pistols were Klee's business. Revolvers and automatics, and, occasionally, shotguns and rifles. Just twice in his career he had been asked for machine guns, and both times he'd been able to supply the order. Both times the customer had had to wait a bit, but Amos Klee had eventually supplied the order.

With an ordinary pistol it was easier. Same day service. Call him in the morning—drop in in the afternoon, and pick up the merchandise. Simple. And later on, if you wanted, Klee would buy the pistol back at the original price. He would then rotate barrel and grip with another pistol, clean it, relube it, if necessary, and sell it again. If he was offered a pistol he hadn't had in stock before, he'd buy it at a very low price, less than a quarter what he would eventually ask for it, because with a gun new to him there was the additional work of filing the serial numbers away. As a sideline, he did a small business in fake collector's items. He had done three of four Dance Bros. & Park .44 cap-and-ball revolvers that only an expert with a magnifying glass could prove false.

Because Klee's telephone had been tapped once and he had come close to losing license, permits, and all, during the call Handy had made from Binghamton this morning he hadn't mentioned guns at all.

"Klee speaking."

"Mister Klee, you don't know me, but Dr. Hall of Green Bay recommended you to me. I intend to be in Syracuse next Monday afternoon, and if you're free, I'd like to discuss a matter of some delicacy with you."

"On Monday?"

"Or later today."

"Monday would be best. What's the problem?"

"Well, I'd rather discuss that in person."

"Is it divorce work?"

"Well, yes."

"I'm sorry, I don't handle divorce work."

Handy had apologized, and hung up. Mentioning Dr. Hall of Green Bay had told Klee that he was a customer for a pistol. And Klee demanded that all pistol customers suggest two times when they could drop in to see him, and the one he said *no* to would be the one when they should arrive. If his phone was being tapped again, and if the law ever did catch on to the Dr. Hall from Green Bay gambit, he wanted to be sure he was raided on the wrong day.

So Klee was in, and waiting for them. The old man in the elevator grumbled to himself as he took them up to the third floor, and when they were getting out he said, "I go home six o'clock. You hang around too long, you'll have to walk down."

They ignored him and went down the hall. The same green paint covered the plaster walls here. Klee's office was flanked on one side by a food broker and on the other by a novelty company. Handy led the way into Klee's office.

It was a one-room office with a wooden railing across at mid-point to create the illusion that the area behind it was a private office, the area in front, a reception-and-waiting room. Klee was alone at his cluttered desk at the rear of the office. He was very short and very fat with wire-framed spectacles and lifeless black hair. The front of his suit was littered with cigarette ashes. He had a surprisingly shy smile and a fond sensual way of handling guns.

It had often occurred to his customers that Klee was a setup to be robbed. Go in to buy a gun, buy it, turn it around and hold Klee up, then walk out. Klee would think twice before squawking to the law. But most of Klee's customers liked him, admired his merchandise, and trusted his discretion, so they chose other targets instead.

Besides, there was a story: One time, a young hotshot had decided to hold Klee up, but he'd talked about it too much and the word had got back to Klee. The kid made a call, and when he came in to get the gun Klee gave it to him. He checked it. It was loaded, so he turned it around and told Klee to get his hands up. Instead, Klee reached for another gun. The hotshot hadn't intended to kill him, but it looked as though he'd have to, so he pulled the trigger and the gun blew up in his hand, mangling it badly. Klee had laughed and asked if the hotshot wanted him to call the Police Rescue Squad? The hotshot stuffed his ruined hand into his coat pocket and ran out. Klee never heard of him again. Nobody else ever tried to hold him up.

Klee waved from the desk, calling "Come on in! Handy, it's you! I thought I recognized the voice, but I couldn't quite place it."

"How you doing, Amos?"

"Not bad, not bad. Got a nice one for you, Handy, a real nice one." He glanced over at Parker. "I'm sorry," he said. "Do I know you?"

"It's Parker, Amos," Handy said. He was grinning. "He had his face done over."

"Well, I'll be! I'd never recognize you." His smile faded. "You wanted two guns? I'm sorry, I didn't catch it, Handy. You should have said, 'My partner and I,' or something like that."

"I've already got a gun," Parker told him. "I got down south, I didn't know I'd be coming through here."

"Oh, that's all right. You'll buy from me again."

"Sure."

Klee struggled up from his desk now, showing himself to be even shorter and fatter than he'd looked while sitting down. He turned toward the old iron safe in the corner. "I suppose you're in a hurry."

Handy said, "The elevator operator's in a hurry."

"He's getting worse every day, that old man. One of these days, he'll refuse to run the elevator at all, and maybe *then* they'll fire him. Maybe."

Klee smiled over his shoulder at them, then crouched down in front of the safe to work the combination. His chubby fingers spun the dial back and forth, he pushed the handle down, and the safe opened. He removed a flat wooden box, of the kind jewelers keep particularly precious necklaces in, and brought it over to the desk.

"A real nice piece," he said, opening the box. "Iver Johnson, model 66, snub. She'll take .38 S & W or Colt New Police, five shots. The rear sight has been removed, and she's got new plastic grips."

He took the revolver from the box—the box was lined
with green velvet—and held it tenderly in his hands. His
hands and the gun were short and stubby. His hands fon-
dled the gun as he talked about it. "You see the rounded
front sight? Won't catch in your pocket like the Cadet.
They call this one the Trailsman. Nice and small, handy
for pocket or purse, like they say." He giggled, and reluctantly handed the gun over to Handy.

Handy looked it over. "This the best you got?"

"For the price, for the size, yes. In a revolver. Now, if
you want an automatic, I've got a nice Starfire .380, seven
shots. She's not quite as small as this, but, of course, thinner."

"What do you want for this one?"

"Seventy."

"And the automatic?"

"Eighty."

"This one's okay."

"She's a very nice little revolver, she really is." Klee
closed the safe, leaving the box out. "I've sold her twice before, and never any complaints."

"That's good. You've got ammunition?"

"Of course." Klee went back to his desk, sat down, and
opened the bottom right-hand drawer. He took a small box
of cartridges out and set it on the desk.

Handy didn't bother to load the revolver. He stowed it
away inside his hunting jacket, put the box of cartridges in
his pants pocket, and started to pay Klee for the gun.

But Parker objected. "No. I'm financing this one, remember?"

"Oh. Sure."

Parker counted the money out into Klee's desk.

Klee watched, smiling, and then said, "Remember now, I'll buy her back when you're done with her. Half-price. Thirty-five dollars, if you want to bring her back."

"If we get the chance," Handy promised.

"That's good, that's good. And you, too, Parker. I'll take yours off your hands when you're finished with it. What is it?"

"Smith & Wesson, .38, short barrel."

"Model 10?"

"I think so."

Klee considered. "If it's in good condition I can give you twenty for it."

"All right," said Parker. "If we pass through on the way back."

"Of course. I'll be seeing you."

"So long."

3

Handy pointed. "That one," he said. "To the left of the building with the neon."

Parker looked at the house where Bronson lived and nodded. He pulled the Olds over to the curb and stopped, then gazed across at the mass of stone.

It was Saturday night. A thousand miles away, the Club Cockatoo was being robbed, but Parker didn't know that yet. Neither did Bronson, who would get a call about it later that night.

Parker shut off the engine. "Let's go for a walk."

"Right."

They got out of the car. The park was beside them; they walked along it, not crossing till they were opposite the next cross street. They went down the cross street, and turned right, and walked along toward the rear of Bronson's house. They walked slowly, casually, two big men in hunting jackets

and caps, their hands in their pockets, not speaking to each
other. They weren't going in after Bronson tonight, this walk
was just to have a look around.

Handy murmured, "There's the garage."

"Driveway, there."

They strolled along, looking in all the parked cars they
passed, studying the driveways as they went by. They continued to the next corner, then turned back toward the park
again.

Handy said, "It's wide open. Does that figure?"

"Maybe Bronson's got a front around here, so it would look
funny for him to have guards at the driveways."

"I guess so."

"He'll have them in there with him, though."

Parker thought about it as they walked along. This was
Bronson's front, Bronson's cover. He probably had his life here
completely separated from his life in the Outfit—like Handy
with his diner in Presque Isle, Maine, or Parker when he was
being Charles Willis. Maybe Bronson figured this Buffalo
cover was enough to protect him.

So this should tie the score. Bronson breaks into Charles
Willis; Parker breaks into Buffalo.

They turned right, walked past the front of Bronson's
place, and on to the end of the block. Then they crossed over
to the park again, walked back to the car, climbed in, and
Parker drove away.

So that was Bronson's hideout. A big pile of stones, set
back from the street, the grounds surrounded by high hedges.

Neighbors far away on both sides. Looking at it from the park, on the right, there was a school for the blind; on the left, some fraternal organization's meetinghouse. Both sides empty at night, anyway. The deserted park across the street. And nothing but his own garage in back. Bronson was isolated in there, a sitting duck. You could set off dynamite, and no one would hear a thing.

"You want days or nights?" Handy asked.

"I'll take nights. I slept this afternoon on the way in."

"Okay."

They headed north, through Kenmore and Tonawanda, and found a motel near the thruway. The woman in the office talked all the time, reminding Parker of Madge, except she was fat. She finally showed them their unit and gave them the key and went away. Parker and Handy carried their luggage inside.

Handy looked at his watch. "Ten o'clock. I'll see you at ten in the morning."

"Right."

Parker went back to the car, drove south again into Buffalo, and over to Bronson's house. He parked across the street and down the block a way so that he was facing the house. His watch told him it was ten-thirty.

He got pencil and notebook out of the glove compartment and made a rough sketch of the front of the house, numbering the windows from one to eleven. Five of the windows were lighted. He wrote: *10:20—1–2–3–6–7*. He had passed the rear of the house coming in, and there had been no lights on back there at all.

The notes finished, he put the pencil and notebook down on the seat beside him, lit a cigarette, and settled down to wait.

At eleven-forty, a prowl car went by, headed east. Parker jotted it down.

At eleven-fifty-five, window 3 went out. At eleven-fifty-seven, window 9 lit up. He wrote it down. At twelve-ten, window 9 went out. He noted that.

At twelve-twenty windows 6 and 7 went off. Parker waited, but no other lights went on to replace them. He started the car and drove around the block, but there still weren't any lights on in back. He returned to his parking space.

At one-fifteen, the prowl car went by again, once more headed east. So it was a belt, and not a back-and-forth deal. The belt took about an hour and a half. Parker wrote it down.

After the prowl car disappeared from his rearview mirror, he got out of the Olds and crossed the street. The street lights were widely spaced here and all of them were on the park side. He was only a shadow when he slipped through the opening in the hedge and moved at an angle across the lawn toward the lighted windows. He peered over a sill at the room inside.

An oval oak table, with a chandelier above, and five men sitting around the table. It took Parker a minute to figure out what they were doing. Playing some game.

Monopoly. For real money, one-cent to the dollar.

Parker studied them and picked out Bronson right away. He had a rich, irritated, overfed look. The other four had the stolid truculence of club fighters, strike-breakers or body-guards. In this case, bodyguards. As Parker watched, Bronson bought Marvin Gardens.

Parker moved away from the window, around the house, keeping close to the wall. There was an apartment over the garage, which he hadn't noticed before. There was a light on up there, and record-player music came softly from the open window. As Parker watched, a Negro in an undershirt showed in the window. The chauffeur, undoubtedly. Parker continued around the house.

There were no other lights on. Someone had gone to bed in the room behind window 9. The chauffeur was in his apart-ment over the garage. Bronson and four bodyguards were playing Monopoly downstairs. The one who had gone to bed, Bronson's wife? Probably. So there were six in the house, plus the chauffeur. Parker went back to the car and wrote it all down in the notebook.

Two-fifty, the prowl car again.

Three-ten, window 3 went on. A minute later it went off again, then an upstairs pair of windows, 6 and 7, went on. They stayed on.

Who would have left the game? Bronson. Window 3 would have shown the light he'd turned on to go upstairs. Windows 6 and 7 were probably his bedroom. Windows 1 and 2, where the game was, stayed on.

Three forty-five, windows 6 and 7 went off. Then window

8 came on, stayed on for five minutes, and went off. So, was 8 Bronson's bedroom? Maybe he had a den or something upstairs, and he'd spent some time there before going to bed. Parker wrote it down, then added a question mark.

He drove around the block again. The chauffeur's light was out, and there were still no lights on in the back of the house.

The bodyguards didn't even cover the back of the house. They were still in front, playing Monopoly.

Parker didn't believe it. He parked around in front again, left the car, and went over to the house to check. And there they were, all four of them, still playing Monopoly at the oval oak table.

Parker went back to the car. He wrote it down and put an exclamation point after it.

When window 3 went on at four-fifty, and windows 1 and 2 went off, he knew they were all going to bed. None of them would stay up all night, to be sure. They would all go to bed. When window 3 went black Parker started the Olds, and drove around to the back of the house. A row of lights came on on the third floor. He waited until they went off, one by one.

Now the entire house was in darkness. There was no one awake to give an alarm. Parker went back to his parked car and settled down to wait for morning. He noted the prowl car's infrequent but regular passage, and also that the two cops in it never gave him a second glance. He'd been sitting here all night, but they hadn't bothered him.

At seven-thirty, he put pencil and notebook in his pocket,

left the Olds, and walked into the park. There was a black-top path with some benches along it. He sat on one, bundled up in the hunting jacket, and chain-smoked while he watched the house and waited for ten o'clock.

At five past nine, a black Cadillac came out through the opening in the hedge, and turned right. Squinting, Parker could see the Negro chauffeur at the wheel and one man in back. That would be Bronson. Another black Cadillac came out from the cross street to the left, turned, and fell in behind the first one. There were four men in it. The two Cadillacs drove away. So now there would be no one in the house except Bronson's wife.

At nine-thirty, a cab stopped in front of the house and a Negro woman got out, carrying a brown paper bag. She went into the house. Cook or maid or cleaning woman, her work clothes in a bag.

At five minutes to ten, another cab came along and stopped, this one pulling to the curb behind the Olds. Handy got out and paid the driver. Parker got to his feet and strolled along the path, looking over at Handy. Handy checked the Olds first, then looked around until he spied Parker. He came towards him, across the grass. Parker sat down on the nearest bench.

Handy sat down next to him. "How'd it go?"

Parker got out the notebook and read off what had happened in the past twelve hours, with his own commentary and explanations. Handy listened, nodding, and said, "He's making it easy for us."

"It doesn't figure."

"Sure it does. He thinks he's safe here. The bodyguards are for just-in-case, but he doesn't really think he'll need them."

"We'll go in Thursday. That'll give us five days to double-check."

"Okay."

Parker got to his feet. "See you tonight."

"Right."

Parker looked over at the Olds. "Maybe we ought to move the car."

"I won't need it till after dark."

"I'll be right back."

Parker went over and got into the car and drove it away. He took it halfway around the park, locked it, and walked back through the park to Handy. "It's over there. You follow the path straight through."

"Okay."

Parker gave him the keys then walked out of the park. He found a cab, and went back to the motel.

4

Wednesday afternoon, Parker phoned Bett Harrow in Miami. She wasn't in her room so he had her paged, dropping dimes and quarters into the phone while he waited. Handy was in Buffalo, sitting in the park across from Bronson's house, a job that had become considerably dull by now. Bronson spent most of his time at home, and had no visitors. Parker's estimate of the household and the position of particularly important rooms had been verified over and over again.

There was only one reason for watching the house now. Bronson might decide to leave, might suddenly pack his luggage, and go off to some other city. Handy had suggested going in before Thursday since the job seemed simpler than they could have hoped for, but Parker wanted to wait. He wanted to be sure the Outfit had been hit a few times before he got rid of Bronson. So they waited, and continued the monotonous job of watching Bronson's house. Hardly anything was written in the notebook anymore.

If things went right, he could be back in Florida by Friday or Saturday. That was why he was calling Bett Harrow, to be sure she would still be there and that she still had the gun. If she'd gotten tired of waiting and had already turned it over to the law, he wanted to know that, too.

When she finally came on the line, he said, "This is Chuck."

"Oh! Where are you?"

"Not in Florida. You still got the gun?"

"It was very clever of you to figure out why I took it."

"No it wasn't. There couldn't be any other reason."

"I might have just wanted a gun." He could hear the sardonic smile in her voice.

"Yeah. Do you still have it?"

"Of course. You asked me to wait a month, didn't you?"

"All right. I'll be back in a couple of days. Figure to see me in your room sometime Saturday night."

"Sounds exciting."

"Yeah." He hung up and left the phone booth.

The booth was in the gas station, across the road from the motel. Parker went out to the road, waited for a break in the traffic, then strode across. It was six-fifteen; the rush hour traffic was lessening. Parker went into his motel room and stretched out on the bed to wait for ten o'clock.

He was oddly tense and impatient. He didn't like this feeling, he hadn't expected it. Always, when he was working, when the job was being set up and he was waiting for it to start, when everything was planned and ready, and all he had to do was look at the clock and wait for it to tell him *now*— always, during that time, he felt compact and timeless, almost bodiless, without impatience or tension or boredom or nervousness of any kind. One time, in Spokane, he was on a warehouse job, and he'd had to sit in silent darkness inside a truck for six hours, not even able to smoke, and he'd done it with no trouble at all. It was while working, while a job was being set up and run through, that he felt most alive and most calm.

Except this time. This time he couldn't get into the mood. This time he wasn't finding the calm satisfaction in planning the job.

Because it wasn't any ordinary job, that was why, and he knew it. This wasn't money he was after, it was a man. It wasn't for profit, it was personal reasons. He felt strange using the methods and experience of his work for personal reasons.

He found himself thinking of Bett Harrow. He would bed her Saturday night, first thing. Before talking about the gun and whatever demands she had to make, before any business at all. Do it right away, because there might be bitterness later, and he wouldn't want it spoiled by bitterness.

At least, in this way, towards sex, he was reacting as though on a normal job. He never had a craving for a woman while working, not an immediate, right-now, sort of craving. It was part of his pattern, part of the way he lived. Immediately after a job, he was always insatiable, satyric, like a groom on a honeymoon after a long and honorable engagement. Gradually, the pace would slacken, the pressure would ease, and the need would grow less fierce, until, by the time the next job came along, he was an ascetic again. He wouldn't touch a woman or even think much about women until that job was over. But once a job was completed, the cycle would start again.

It had always been that way. When Lynn, his wife, had been alive, it had been a tough pattern for her to get used to, but now that Lynn was dead, he worked out his cycle on the bodies of transients like Bett Harrow, which was easier for all concerned.

Saturday, he knew, he would be raring. So it would have to be pleasure before business that night.

He had been lying on the bed, thinking, but now he got to his feet and paced around the room. His damn impatience was gnawing at him, keeping him from resting. He looked at his watch. It was only twenty-five minutes to seven. He shrugged back into his coat and left the motel, headed for the diner, wondering how long he could make dinner last.

Just until tomorrow night. Take it easy, he told himself. One more night.

5

Handy gnawed at a wooden match. "I don't like wasting time on the chauffeur."

They were parked in front of Bronson's house, against the opposite curb. Parker was at the wheel, Handy beside him. It was ten-forty, Thursday night.

Parker said, "The chauffeur's the only one outside the main house. They're liable to have a phone to him back there or something like that. If one of them gets word to him, there's no way we can stop him sending for help."

"I suppose so," Handy agreed doubtfully.

"Besides, his windows overlook the back of the house, and that's the way we'll be going in."

"Yeah, you're right." Handy shook his head and threw a match away. "I'm not used to this idea, breaking into a *house*. I'll keep my mouth shut and let you do the planning."

This was the second time they'd disagreed and Handy had

admitted being wrong. The first time, Handy had wanted to wait till three or four in the morning, when the whole crowd would be asleep, but Parker had explained to him what was wrong with that.

"That way, there's six of them in six different rooms, and a silent house. It'd take us too long to get them all squared away. If we wait till the Monopoly game's on and Bronson's wife is watching television in that little room on the right and Bronson is up in his den, we've got six people in three rooms, a house with enough noise in it so we can move around, and the only person on the second floor is the one we're after. We won't have to brace the bodyguards at all. We can by-pass them and go straight for Bronson. Just so we keep an eye on the stairs, that's all."

That last point, about by-passing the bodyguards, was what had mulled around in Handy's head for the last few hours. If they were going to ignore the bodyguards, why not ignore the chauffeur, too?

Now that had been straightened out, and they were in agreement. Parker looked over at the house. "There goes the light on in the den. It's time."

"Right."

They got out of the Olds and walked down the street on the park side, strolling, like friends out for a constitutional. Tonight, both wore topcoats, snug-fitting, to allow freedom of movement, and hats tilted back from their foreheads. Their shoes were rubber-soled and rubber-heeled. They had their hands in their topcoat pockets. Their guns were in their right-hand topcoat pockets.

Now that the time had finally come, Parker felt his tension draining away. At long last, the peace of working hours was spreading through him. It could take an hour to walk around the block; it wouldn't matter. He was patient, and calm, and certain.

They crossed over, went down the dim cross street, turned right. This narrow street was lit only at the intersections, leaving a pool of darkness in the middle, where the rear driveway to Bronson's house was. They walked down that way, their shoes silent on the sidewalk, and then slipped through the hedge onto Bronson's grounds. The black-top muffled their steps, too; they would have had to be more cautious with gravel.

To their right was the four-car garage. An outside stairway up the far side led to the apartment above. Parker and Handy, guns now in their hands, hurried across the face of the garage, and then moved slowly and cautiously up the white wooden stairs. The sky was blanketed by cloud masses; it was a moonless, starless, black night. The white stairs were vague gray shapes in the darkness.

At the top was a landing with a door. There was a four-paned window in the door, covered with thick curtains, so that only a vague hint of light came through.

Parker rapped on the door. A sudden startled voice from inside called, "Just a second!"

Parker raised an eyebrow, surprised. He'd expected the

chauffeur to ask who it was, and he'd intended saying that
Bronson wanted to see him. Which should have been enough
to make the chauffeur open the door. The guns would have
done the rest, keeping the chauffeur quiet while they went in
and tied and gagged him. But the chauffeur hadn't asked anything at all. Which maybe meant he was expecting somebody.
Parker glanced toward the house, but saw nothing. No lights
were on in the rear of the house; no one was coming toward
the garage.

He'd have to make sure, once they got inside.

The door opened and the chauffeur stood there, wearing
black trousers, an undershirt, and brown slippers. He looked
at them, at the guns in their hands, took a step backward, crying "Oh, my God!" He looked as though he were going to
faint. He made no attempt to shut the door again.

Parker had the crazy feeling the chauffeur had been expecting him, that he, Parker, was the one the chauffeur had
been waiting for.

The chauffeur's face was curiously mottled. He kept backing away across the room, shaking his head, gesturing wildly,
and murmuring, "My God, my God! I knew it, I knew it. My
God, I knew it—"

Parker walked in and to the right, and Handy came in after
him, shutting the door. Parker said, "Take it easy. Don't get
excited, just take it easy."

But the chauffeur kept backing away and muttering to
himself, until he ended up against the far wall. He stood

there, shaking his head, terrified out of his wits, his hands still making vague, half-formed movements.

They were in the living room. It was nicely set up with modern furniture and pole lamps and a large stereo rig against one wall.

Handy was frowning at the chauffeur, just as baffled as Parker. "What's the matter with you?" He looked at Parker. "What the hell's the matter with him?"

"I knew it," mumbled the chauffeur. "I knew it, I knew it, my God, I knew it! Why didn't I have some sense, why didn't I—"

"I don't know," said Parker. "You. Shut up."

The chauffeur immediately shut up. He brought his hands to his sides and kept them there. He stood at a sort of ragged attention, leaning backwards against the wall.

And then all of a sudden Parker understood. He laughed and said, "Watch him, Handy. I'll be right back."

"Sure thing."

"Mister," said the chauffeur. His voice was hoarse. He sounded as though he were going to start pleading.

"Just shut up a minute, friend." Parker walked on by him.

Beyond the living room was a dining room and a hall that led to a kitchen, with a bedroom and bathroom off that to the right. Parker went to the bedroom door and turned the knob. It was locked.

"All right, come on out." When nothing happened, he said, "Nobody's going to hurt you, come on out. If I have to shoot the lock off, you won't like it."

A key grated in the lock, and the door was opened hesitantly. The woman who came, reluctant and blinking, from the dark bedroom was short and somewhat plump, and sour-looking. She was probably in her early thirties, and wore the kind of black dress women wear to cheap bars. Her hair was dyed a brassy blond, and her skin was white.

"He forced me," she said, looking at Parker's chest rather than his face. She had a twangy voice and sullenness riddled it. "I didn't wanna come up here. He forced me."

"Sure. Come on along."

"It's the truth," she insisted sullenly.

Parker took her elbow and led her back to the living room. When Handy saw her, he grinned in sudden understanding. He turned to the chauffeur. "Is *that* what you were worried about?"

"He forced me," repeated the woman sullenly. She said it as though it were something she'd memorized for a pageant she hadn't wanted to be a part of anyway.

Handy shook his head, grinning. "Listen," he said to the chauffeur. "You weren't planning on going to *school* with her up here, were you?"

The chauffeur blinked and stared at him.

"It'll go hard on you if you were figuring on studying geometry with her or anything contaminating like that," Handy said to him. "Were you?"

The chauffeur was getting his own complexion back. He essayed a small smile in answer to Handy's grin and shook his head.

"That's all right, then," said Handy. "Just so you weren't figuring on learning anything."

The chauffeur's smile faded away again, as he stared at the gun in Handy's hand.

"This doesn't have anything to do with you," Handy told him. "Or with the woman."

"He forced me."

"Shut up," Parker said.

Handy said, "We're going in after Bronson, that's all. And we thought it might be a good idea to just tie you up to keep you out of trouble."

"Well, I'll be damned," said the chauffeur. "Well, I'll be double-die-damned."

"So you and the lady lie down on the floor," Handy told him.

"I didn't wanna come up here."

Parker knocked her down. "You're supposed to lie down on the floor," he said.

She started to snuffle.

The chauffeur stretched out on the floor, seeming relieved at the chance to get off his feet. Parker stood covering the two of them while Handy went to get something to tie them.

The chauffeur looked up and said, "You going to kill him?"

"Probably. You'll have to find a new job for yourself."

"You going to kill her, too?"

"His wife? No."

"Then I won't have to look for a new job. Just make sure

you tie me good and tight, so she'll know I couldn't of got
loose and warned him."

"What's the matter? Don't you like him?"

"He's a royal son of a bitch."

"That's right," Parker said.

Handy came back with a ball of heavy twine and two extension cords. He used the twine to secure their hands behind
their backs, and the extension cords to tie their ankles together. He had found undershirts in a drawer of the dresser
and he used these to gag them.

When the two of them were tied and gagged, Parker went
through the apartment turning off the lights. Then he and
Handy went out to the landing, shutting the door behind
them. They went down the stairs and crossed the black-top
toward the dark hulk of the house.

"The poor bastard," said Handy, speaking softly. "We sure
picked the wrong night."

6

Handy had three small, slender tools wrapped in flannel tucked inside his topcoat. He took them out now and unwrapped them. It was pitch-black at the rear of the house, but Handy could see with his hands. His tools made muted, metallic sounds against the lock on the back door and then the door came open as though the lock had been made of butter. Handy wrapped his tools up again, tucked them inside his topcoat, and took his .38 back out of his pocket.

Parker went in first. He had his gun in his right hand, a pencil flash in his left. There was electric tape over the tip of the flash, leaving only a small opening for the light to peep through.

They had entered a stairwell. Concrete stairs led down to the basement, wooden stairs led to the upper floors. Straight ahead was another door, unlocked. Parker opened it cautiously, to find more darkness. He aimed the light into the darkness and saw that they were in a big, square kitchen. He crossed it, Handy behind him, and on the other side there were three doors. One led to a small dining room on the right, one to a deep pantry, and the third to a hallway. At the far end of the hallway, there was light. As Parker started down the hallway, clocks all over the house began striking eleven.

They waited for the clocks to finish, unmoving. When the chiming ended, Handy whispered, "Jesus!"

Parker started forward again, and another chime sounded. He thought at first it was another clock, then he realized it must be the front door. "Hold it," he whispered.

Ahead, at the far end of the hallway, one of the bodyguards went by. They waited, heard the front door open, heard voices, then a door closed and the bodyguard went back to the Monopoly game.

Parker moved again. The two of them hurried silently down the hallway to where it opened into the main front hall. Someone was going upstairs. They heard a casual voice. "Hello, Mr. Bronson. A real mess, that Cockatoo situation."

Another voice muttered something unintelligible.

"Very nice house, Mr. Bronson. Really very fine. Really."

"You said that last time."

That would be Bronson. He sounded bitter about something.

"I must mean it, then."

"Yeah. Well, Quill, come on into the office."

There was silence, and then a door closed upstairs.

Parker whispered, "Watch the stairs."

Handy nodded.

Parker moved to the right, at an angle, and came to the doorway where the bodyguards were playing Monopoly. He glanced in, saw them sitting there, concentrating on the game. They would be there another three or four hours. They played Monopoly all the time, as though they were addicted to it. They could be ignored.

Parker hadn't expected a visitor. Bronson had had only one visitor in the five days they'd been watching his house, and that had been a youngish man with a briefcase who'd showed up in a chauffeur-driven limousine Sunday night. He'd looked like an insurance adjustor, except for the limousine. He'd stayed half an hour, and then had gone away again.

He wondered if this were the same one, back again. Whether it was or not, he was holding things up.

Parker went back to Handy and whispered, "They're at the game again. We can forget them."

"Right."

Mrs. Bronson was already in bed. They'd seen the light go on and off in her bedroom an hour before. So, except for the visitor, everything was set up the way they'd planned.

Parker led the way up the stairs. They were thickly carpeted, as was the hall on the second floor, so they moved without sound.

The third door on the right should be Bronson's office. Bronson's bedroom was beyond that, and his wife's bedroom further down, at the end. The hall was dimly lit by electric candelabras. Light gleamed under the door of Bronson's office.

Parker moved up silently to the door and pressed his ear against it. He heard the stranger's voice, a monotone. After a minute, he figured out what the stranger was talking about. His name was Quill. There'd been a hit at a place called the Club Cockatoo and he was describing the robbery to Bronson.

Parker smiled to himself. He'd been right. He wondered which of his letters had set off the robbery. He moved away from the door, back down the hall to Handy, who was waiting at the head of the stairs. Handy was keeping an eye on the staircase, just in case anyone decided to come up.

Parker whispered, "The guy is called Quill. They're talking about a robbery."

Handy grinned. "Just *one?*"

"I don't know."

Parker went back and listened some more. Bronson didn't like Quill very much. Quill was explaining how come the people who worked at the Club Cockatoo had let the robbers get away with it. Parker listened, as impatient as Bronson, and at last Quill said, "Well, I think we may have learned from this."

Bronson's voice said bitterly, "And the others?"

"I'd heard there'd been some more."

"*Eleven* more."

Parker moved away, back to Handy, smiling again. "Twelve," he whispered. "They been knocked over twelve times."

"That must have hurt," said Handy.

"Karns will go along now. Twelve times! He'll pay us to stop."

Handy looked over the rail at the stairs and the hallway below. Faintly, the Monopoly players could still be heard. Handy said, "What do you want to do? Tackle him with that guy in there?"

"No. He's maybe due some place else after he leaves here. We don't want to keep him and louse up his schedule."

"What, then?"

"We'll wait. In Bronson's bedroom."

"Right."

They went down the hall together, past the den door, through which they could faintly hear the murmuring of Quill and Bronson. Parker went in first, shining the pencil flash around, reassuring himself the room was empty. Handy came in after him. Parker shut off the flashlight, and they settled down to wait.

They left the hall door partly open, just in case one of the bodyguards should come up, or Mrs. Bronson should decide to leave her room. They took their hats off and tossed them on the bed, but kept their topcoats on. Handy sat on the edge of the bed, and Parker stood by the door. They could hear Bronson and Quill talking next door, but couldn't quite make out the words. They both had their guns in their hands.

They waited about fifteen minutes and then they heard the den door open. "Good night, Mr. Bronson." Bronson muttered something from inside and Quill shut the office door and walked away toward the stairs.

Parker whispered, "Take the stairs. I'm going in after Bronson now."

"Right."

As soon as Quill started down the stairs and was out of sight, Handy moved out of the bedroom. He went silently down the hall and stood against the wall by the head of the stairs, covering them.

Parker waited a minute, then went down the hall and opened the door to Bronson's den. Bronson was standing at the window looking out, his back to the door. Parker studied his back, wondering if there were any reason to spend time talking to Bronson first, and had just about decided there wasn't any reason to, when Bronson turned around.

Bronson saw him, and gave a start, but recovered quickly. A bitter smile creased his lips and he said, "So you're Parker."

"That's right." Parker raised the .38.

But there was sudden motion to his right. He turned his head and saw Handy coming on the run. He stepped into the den, and Handy barreled in after him, saying hoarsely, "They're coming back up!"

Parker turned to Bronson. "Why?"

"What? Quill's staying the night."

"All right. Keep your mouth shut."

Bronson shook his head. "No. I've been wondering if those bodyguards were any damn good. Now I'll find out." He raised his head and shouted, "Help!"

Parker shot in irritation and ducked back out the hall. Behind him, Bronson sagged onto the desk.

Quill and one of the bodyguards were at the head of the stairs. They gaped at Parker and Handy, then turned to run back down again. Parker and Handy fired, but they'd both aimed at the bodyguard, so Quill got away, stumbling over the body which was rolling down the stairs.

"The wife!" said Parker. "Shut her up."

"Right."

Handy hurried down the hall and Parker went back into Bronson's den. Bronson was lying on his face behind the desk. Parker checked him, but he wouldn't need a booster. He straightened and took the phone off the hook, hoping there was only one trunk line in the house. If all the extensions were on the same line, no calls could be made.

Parker hurried back to the hall. Handy hadn't come back yet. Parker ran down to the end, by the stairs, just in time to see the three bodyguards starting up. He fired, not hitting anybody, and they ducked back into the room where they'd been playing Monopoly. Parker knelt behind the railing and waited for Handy.

This was a good spot, for right now. Looking over the railing he could see straight down to the foot of the stairs, and across the main hall to the front door. He could also see the room where the bodyguards and Quill were holed up. He could keep them in there, unless they tried going out the window.

Somebody took a shot at him from the doorway down

there. He ducked back, waited a beat, and leaned forward in time to see one of them making a dash across the hall for the room on the opposite side, hoping to catch Parker and Handy in a cross fire. Parker slid the nose of the .38 over the top of the railing, dropped the running man, and ducked back out of sight again. They were firing from the room on the right again, the bullets gouging the wall over Parker's head.

Handy showed up, running in a crouch, ducking down to kneel beside Parker. "Tied and gagged," he said. "What now?"

"Three left. Two bodyguards and Quill."

"What about the back stairs?"

"I don't want a chase. We finish them off in here. It's private in here. No neighbors, no questions."

"Okay."

"Besides, we want time to go through the place. You don't want to do this for nothing."

"Okay."

"Yeah, that's right."

"You stay here. Take a shot at them every once in a while. I'll go down and around outside to the window."

"Right."

Parker slid away in a crouch and straightened when he was part way down the hall. He hurried to the far end, where he found the stairs that led to the back door. He started down them, and a sound made him stop. Somebody was coming in through the back door.

Parker waited. Whoever it was, he was being slow and cautious. Occasional faint noises told Parker where he was and what he was doing. He came in the back door, shut it carefully behind him, and then started up the stairs. Parker had shut the second-floor door behind him, so it was inky black in the stairwell. He sat on the top step, the .38 in his right hand and the pencil flash in his left, waiting. Both were aimed down at the landing.

The man came slowly up the stairs, and finally reached the landing. He made the turn and started up the other half-flight toward Parker. Parker switched on the pencil flash. It was one of the bodyguards, staring up at him, blinded by the light. Parker fired, and the face fell away. He switched off the light and heard the bodyguard go crashing back down the stairs.

Parker followed him, hurrying. He'd been delayed too long. Handy would be wondering where the hell he was.

He went out the back door and around the outside of the house. He saw the open window the bodyguard had crawled through, trying Parker's tactic in reverse. He moved up to the window, peered over the edge, and saw the two men inside. The remaining bodyguard was crouched by the doorway, peering out around the corner, an automatic in his hand. Quill was at the far end of the room, sitting in a leather chair, the briefcase on his lap. He had the blank expression of somebody in a waiting room.

Parker called to the bodyguard, "Drop the gun. Don't turn around."

But the bodyguard wouldn't quit. He spun around, firing

wildly, and Parker dropped him with one shot. Then he
turned and showed the gun to Quill, resting it on the window
sill. "Don't move," he said. "Don't make any move at all."

"I'm just sitting here," Quill answered. He didn't act particularly worried.

"Handy! Come on down."

They waited, and, after a minute Handy came in, grinning.
He looked around and said, "One more. There's one missing."

"I met him on the back stairs. Watch this guy Quill."

"Right."

Parker left the window and went around to the back of the
house again. He entered and walked through the house to the
game room where Handy and Quill were waiting.

Parker went over to Quill. "You know Karns?"

"Not personally. I've heard of him."

"I hear he'll be taking over."

"Bronson's dead?"

"I want you to give Karns a message from me."

"I take it you're Parker."

"That's right."

"And since you want me to deliver a message, that means
you'll let me live?"

"Why not?"

Quill smiled. "Exactly. Why not?"

"You heeled, Quill?"

"A gun? I never carry one."

"I didn't think so. All right, the message. Tell Karns I'll
start getting in touch with my friends, telling them to forget

the Outfit. But it'll take a while. There'll probably be a few more robberies before I can get in touch with everybody. This thing'll be tougher to stop than it was to start. But that was Bronson's doing, making me start it in the first place. I'll stop it as soon as I can. You tell Karns that."

"There may be some more robberies, but you'll stop them as soon as you can?"

"That's it. And tell him, if I have to, I can always start in again. And if I happen to be killed by the Outfit, my friends will even the score." The last was a lie, but Karns couldn't be sure of it.

"I'll tell him."

"Good." Parker turned to Handy. "I'll keep an eye on this bird while you go through the house."

"Right." Handy pocketed his gun and left the room.

"Have you been masterminding these robberies?" Quill asked.

"No. My friends have been doing them on their own."

"They've been very professional robberies."

"My friends are very professional."

"Yes, of course."

They were silent then.

About ten minutes later, Handy came back. "I found a safe," he said. He turned to Quill. "You know anything about it? What he might have in there?"

"No, I'm sorry. I didn't know Mr. Bronson that well."

"I'd hate to take the trouble to go in there and not find

anything but a lot of paper." Handy shrugged. "I'll take the chance."

This time he was gone longer. Parker sat at the table where the bodyguards had been playing Monopoly, and Quill remained in the leather chair, his hands on the briefcase resting on his lap.

Handy was back in half an hour, grinning. "Jackpot," he said. "Bronson must of been holding out on the income tax people. Twenty-four grand in the safe. Plus about three hundred I picked up here and there, and some jewelry. We'll maybe get five or six on the jewelry."

Parker got to his feet. It was over. He could relax. Karns would be more sensible than Bronson. "So long, Quill. Be sure to give Karns the message."

"Yes, I will. Good-by, Mr. Parker."

7

Parker sat at the desk in the motel room writing letters. It was the Green Glen Motel, outside Scranton, and Handy was off having a drink and some of Madge's reminiscence. Parker was copying from the first letter he'd done that afternoon. So far he had finished eight of them.

FRANK,

If you haven't done anything about that first letter I sent you, never mind. I got everything straightened out now, so we can leave the Outfit alone again. I got in touch with the guy who ran the Outfit, and the one who's taking over now has more sense. I talked with him, and we got everything squared away. If you already got the Boston job set up go ahead and do it, but you don't have to on my account. You can always get in

touch with me through Joe Sheer in Omaha. Maybe
we'll work together again some time.

PARKER

He was just starting on the ninth when the door opened.
He looked up, expecting Handy or Madge, but it was Ethel,
Madge's helper, carrying sheets over her arm. "I'm supposed
to change the linen now," she said.

"Go ahead."

She went over to the bed, and he got back to work on the
letters. He did two more. Then she said, "Okay, it's all
changed now."

"That's good."

"Looks nice," she said.

He turned to look at her. She was a hefty girl, with big
mounds for breasts and hips, and rumpled blonde hair framing a face that would have been good-looking if it weren't so
vapid.

"Yeah, very nice. That's good." He wondered if she was
waiting around for a tip.

She said, "You want anything else before I go?"

"No," he said. "That's okay."

She licked her lips and smiled, looking almost animated.
"You sure?"

Then he caught on. And seriously considered it for a second or two, because the job was over and he was feeling the
way he always felt right after a job. It would be a nice break
from the letter-writing to toss this one once, a soft quickie on

the clean sheets. But the blank cowlike face stopped him because he knew there was a blank bovine mind behind it. Tonight, maybe he'd go down into Scranton, though he'd never found much worthwhile in Scranton. If not, he could wait till tomorrow night. Bett Harrow could take care of things. He could save it till then. The first one after a job ought to be a good one, like Bett, not a pig from Scranton. "I'm sure," he said. "Forget it."

"If you say so," she answered. The smile faded and she looked vague and sullen. She went out and closed the door after her.

Parker wrote letters a while longer, and then Handy came in. "Madge'll take care of fencing the jewels for us," he said. "She'll hold onto the dough till the next time we come through. Where you headed next, Parker?"

"I got something waiting for me in Miami."

"Another job?"

"I'm not sure." He told Handy about Bett Harrow, and the gun that had struck Stern on the temple. "I don't know what she wants. If it's something easy, I'll go along with it. Otherwise, the hell with her. It's about time I started building a new cover anyway."

"You want me to come along?"

"What about the diner in Presque Isle, Maine?"

Handy shrugged, grinning sheepishly. "The hell with my diner in Presque Isle, Maine!"

"Come on along, then," Parker said.